The Beauty with Poison 3

——The Unveiling of the Hidden Dagger

Shuang Chenyue

Published by Great Wall Publishing, 2024.

This is a work of fiction. Similarities to real people, places, or events are entirely coincidental.

THE BEAUTY WITH POISON 3 —— The Unveiling of the Hidden Dagger
First edition. May 28, 2024.
Copyright © 2024 Shuang Chenyue.

Written by Shuang Chenyue.

Table of Contents

Volume Three: The Unveiling of the Hidden Dagger

Chapter Thirty: Delight in Your Presence

Timothy envisioned a beautiful future, but reality cruelly dashed his hopes.

The next day, Timothy woke up to find that Abbe had vanished. The vast house was left in disarray, with only Timothy remaining amidst the chaos.

Timothy had no idea when Abbe had left. If not for the mess recalling the wild and intimate scenes of the previous night, he might have thought it was just a dream.

Abbe did not return to Pavilion Arnold; he disappeared like morning dew at dawn. No one knew where he had gone, and he vanished without a trace.

Timothy was disheartened. He had thought that his efforts with the plums had touched Abbe's heart, opening a crack in his tightly shut heart. Despite the impulsive nature of their encounter, Abbe's reactions gave Timothy reason to believe there was something between them.

But Abbe left without a word.

Nevertheless, Timothy couldn't delay any longer due to the uncertain situation in Poiema, which was worrying. He had to put aside his personal matters and embark on his return journey with doubts and concerns.

"Are you worried about Chief Master?" Adam, who was riding in the carriage, noticed Timothy's frown and absent-mindedness, and couldn't help but ask.

Timothy nodded. "Where do you think Abbe might have gone?"

Adam, now dressed in a neat, light blue outfit resembling a clever servant, tilted his head thoughtfully. "Chief Master's hometown is in Euyle. He might have gone there to seek refuge."

"Euyle? Seek refuge? I thought his family was exterminated. Does he still have acquaintances there?"

"The Simpson family was a prominent clan. It's hard to wipe out all connections at once. Besides, Chief Master prefers Sunder over Poiema."

Abbe doesn't like Poiema?

This piqued Timothy's curiosity, prompting him to inquire further.

It turned out that after Payton became an official, he wanted to bring his family to live in Poiema. However, Abbe complained of discomfort and demanded to return to Euyle after just a year. Payton couldn't resist his beloved son and sent him back home. Thus, except for the few months around the New Year, Abbe spent most of his time in Sunder.

"Abbe claimed discomfort in Poiema? Really?"

"Of course not. After spending three months with Chief Master, don't you know his character? He hates being controlled, even by his father," Adam laughed. "It's ironic. Mr. Simpson, a renowned scholar, preached loyalty and filial piety, yet he raised a son who yearns for a free-spirited life and despises fame and fortune."

Timothy finally understood. In Sunder, far from the emperor's reach, Abbe could roam freely and associate with various people. But in Poiema, not only was it close to the emperor, but he also had a strict father at home, making him feel restrained.

"In short, Chief Master isn't a naive child. If he hadn't wandered on his own, he wouldn't have gained so many loyal followers, nor would there have been the later Sabra Village."

"Indeed, he's as free as the wind. My worry for him is truly misplaced..." Timothy sighed with a bitter smile.

"The one misplaced is not you..."

Adam mumbled under his breath.

"Hmm?" Timothy looked at him with wide eyes. "What did you say, Adam?"

"N-nothing!"

Adam quickly lowered his head, embarrassed by his slip of the tongue.

Did he realize his mistake? Adam worried, stealing a glance at Timothy. To his relief, Timothy seemed lost in thought, gazing out of the window, not focused on him.

Adam breathed a sigh of relief, his mind a jumble of thoughts before finally calming down.

Horse hooves clattered as they sped across the fertile plains, soon leaving the Sunder border.

It was midsummer and noon, typically marked by scorching heat. However, the weather this year was unusual. Not long after entering Kamal, a sudden downpour forced them to seek shelter in a nearby county.

After the heavy rain, the temperature dropped drastically. Despite it being June, it felt chillingly cold. By midnight, hail began to fall.

The hailstones, as large as eggs, pelted down fiercely. Lying in the inn, Timothy listened to the hail mixed with the wind, thundering on the roof. The noise was so intense that he wouldn't have been surprised if the roof caved in.

Timothy couldn't sleep all night, and neither did Adam next door. Early the next morning, Timothy stepped out to find Adam yawning, dark circles under his eyes.

The rain had cleared, and Timothy was stunned by the scene outside. Houses were destroyed, rubble was everywhere. Compared to the devastation, their inn was relatively intact, with only a few broken windows, which was a blessing.

The innkeeper, a kind-hearted man, saw the many homeless people shivering in the cold and had his young waiter cook a large pot of porridge for the affected villagers. Timothy and Adam, with nothing else to do, helped the innkeeper. Adam served porridge and water, while Timothy called out on the streets. Soon, a long line formed, with people constantly coming for the porridge, stretching to the end of the street.

"First the drought, then locusts, now hail. How are we supposed to live?"

"It's an ill-fated year. These disasters must be a bad omen."

The crowd murmured in despair, their grievances towards the government clear, though unspoken.

Suddenly, commotion erupted in the crowd. At the back, some kind of disturbance broke out. The sound of galloping hooves grew louder as a group of soldiers on horseback forced their way in, shouting and even arresting and driving people away.

Someone in the crowd yelled, "They're conscripting!" Immediately, the long line dispersed in panic.

"What's happening?" Timothy asked the innkeeper, bewildered.

"Well, they're conscripting labor for the army. Those being taken are former slaves who had recently gained freedom. Originally displaced by famine and war, they became slaves and were sold to warlords. Now that they've settled and started a new life, they're being taken again for military service."

Timothy was still confused. "But there's no war. Where are they being sent?"

"Mausoleum Rudolf," the innkeeper explained patiently. "Since spring, the weather has been unpredictable, even affecting the grasslands up north. With more nomads migrating south and frequent border skirmishes, the government is preparing for worse in autumn by conscripting labor from Kamal."

"Even so, they shouldn't be so oppressive!" Adam, overhearing, was indignant. "They ignore the starving people but are quick to conscript and oppress. What a bunch of scoundrels!"

Seeing Adam's indignation, Timothy quickly covered his mouth. "Adam, be careful. They're the government. It's not something we can meddle in."

"I know," Adam said gloomily. "But seeing those people reminds me of my past... This world, officials are never good!"

"Adam, you were conscripted too?"

Adam's eyes darkened. "I was originally from Tim County, Kamal, and I had an older brother, one year my senior. When I was fourteen, a group of soldiers suddenly burst into our home and took us away, saying we were to be sold in Sunder to raise funds for the army. On the way, those soldiers treated us like animals, often beating us and giving us only watery gruel to eat. I couldn't stand it anymore, so my brother and I escaped halfway. My brother starved to death on the road, and I wandered aimlessly until I finally met Chief Master, who helped me live like a human being."

Adam recounted his harrowing past in a calm tone. His eight-word phrase—"wandering aimlessly, enduring hardships"—barely scratched the surface of the hardships he and his brother endured, leading to his brother's death and leaving Adam alone.

Timothy believed that Adam wasn't the worst off; whether it was Abbe or the other brothers in Sabra Village, their individual tragedies might have been different, but they were all filled with blood and tears.

"Do you miss your brother?" Timothy suddenly asked out of nowhere.

"Of course I do..." Adam looked up at the sky, as if lost in memories. "Although he was only a year older than me, he always looked out for me. He had an endless supply of jokes. Whenever

I felt life was unbearable, he would tell me jokes, making me laugh so hard I couldn't stand."

"He must have loved you very much." Timothy looked at Adam and smiled gently. "I'm an only child, so I've never known what it's like to have siblings. I envy you for having such a good brother."

Adam stared at Timothy for a while, wide-eyed, and said, "I just realized, Alan, when you smile, you look a bit like my brother."

"Really?" Timothy was taken aback, then his smile grew even brighter. "Then I'll smile more for you, Adam."

Adam's face turned crimson. He lowered his eyes awkwardly, scooped a spoonful of white porridge, and nervously put it in his mouth. Strangely, despite the porridge having no seasoning, Adam tasted a hint of sweetness.

To thank Timothy and Adam for their kind help, the generous innkeeper treated them to a hearty meal. After their fill, Timothy and Adam set off again. With most of the remaining journey being mountainous, they abandoned the carriage and rode horses, traversing muddy paths for half a day until they reached a lush valley with babbling brooks.

The rain-washed sky was a vivid blue, and a deep breath brought the fresh scent of grass and earth, lifting Timothy's spirits. Having grown up in Poiema, then spending three months in the drought-stricken Sunder, he savored being surrounded by nature once more, slowing his pace.

In this verdant valley, a shallow river flowed throughout. The clear, emerald water, like a ribbon of blue silk, alternated between gentle and turbulent as it wound through the mountains. Though Adam had wandered the lands of Kamal and Sunder for a year, he had never seen such a breathtaking sight.

"It's like a paradise on earth..."

Adam stood at the edge of a cliff, daringly stretching his neck to look at the river below. The cliff was not very high, only a few meters, but standing at the edge still made his legs feel weak.

"Adam, are you afraid of heights?" Timothy dismounted and walked over to Adam.

"Not really..." Adam hesitated. "Why do you ask?"

Timothy nodded towards the cliff's edge. "Not afraid? Then let's go down and have a look!"

"What? Hey!"

Before Adam could react, Timothy had already jumped down, skillfully navigating the bushes and branches with agility that made one wonder if he was part monkey.

Adam hesitated, unsure whether to follow or stay. Seeing Timothy already at the bottom, waving at him, Adam steeled himself and carefully started his descent.

"It's okay, almost there!"

Originally, Adam was climbing down slowly, but hearing Timothy's encouragement, he lost his focus and slipped, falling straight down.

In that moment, Adam's heart sank. Fortunately, he landed heavily in a strong embrace. Timothy had caught him securely.

"See, I told you it was fine," Timothy said, laughing carelessly.

Adam, however, was so shaken he was covered in cold sweat, his legs trembling so much he couldn't stand, so he crouched by the river, clutching his pounding heart and gasping for breath.

Timothy went to the river, scooped up some water, and took a sip. He felt rejuvenated, as if his entire body had been refreshed.

"Adam, this water is so cool! Come and try it."

"I can't stand up." Adam murmured, holding his ankle.

"Let me see." Timothy approached. "Did you sprain it?"

Without hesitation, Timothy reached for Adam's slender ankle. Caught off guard, Adam's heart raced uncontrollably.

"It's fine..." Timothy examined for a while, seeing no swelling or bruising. He then gently massaged Adam's ankle. "Does this feel better?"

Since that night in Sabra Village, Adam hadn't had the chance to be this close to Timothy. Seizing the rare opportunity, Adam watched Timothy intently while he was focused.

Timothy's nose was a nose, his eyes were eyes, and his eyebrows were eyebrows.

This might sound redundant, but Adam, not well-versed in words, thought it was the best description he could muster.

He had seen handsome men before—Abbe and Penelope, both stunning. Among such beautiful people, Timothy's features weren't the most striking. Yet, for some reason, on Timothy's face, these seemingly ordinary features combined to form an incredibly pleasing appearance, making it hard to look away.

"...Is it because I like him?"

"Hmm?" Timothy suddenly looked up. "Like what?"

Adam's face turned bright red. He hadn't realized he had spoken his thoughts aloud while staring at Timothy.

"I-I mean..." Adam awkwardly withdrew his foot, murmuring, "I..."

Somehow infected by Adam's nervousness, Timothy's heartbeat also quickened. For a moment, neither spoke, their only companions the sound of flowing water and the songs of birds in the empty valley.

Chapter Thirty-One: Bait and Hook

In the end, Adam stammered in front of Timothy for a long time but still couldn't bring himself to say the words "I like you."

Finally, it was Timothy who broke the silence first. He released Adam's ankle, stepped back two paces, and maintained a certain distance from him.

Timothy was afraid of startling Adam, but regardless of his intentions, this distancing added a touch of awkwardness to the silence.

To alleviate the awkwardness, Timothy turned around, his gaze sweeping the surroundings. Suddenly, he noticed something floating on the rapid water, drifting leisurely towards them.

"What's that?"

Timothy walked curiously to the riverbank and picked up the object. It was a shoe. It was unknown which careless person had dropped their shoe in the water. Timothy inspected the shoe closely; it wasn't completely soaked, indicating it had only recently fallen in.

Timothy turned to Adam. "Adam, someone dropped a shoe. The owner should be nearby. You stay here and rest; I'll go and return it."

As soon as Adam heard this, his leg seemed to heal instantly. He jumped up and grabbed Timothy's sleeve. "I want to go too."

Timothy's guess was correct. Following the river upstream for just a quarter of an hour, they found the owner of the shoe—a man dressed in white, sound asleep by the riverside.

Timothy had thought someone so careless to lose a shoe must be a scatterbrained fool, but upon closer inspection, he was amazed.

The man was delicate and handsome, with sharp eyebrows and thin lips, dressed in a moon-white robe, lying quietly on a large boulder by the riverbank. What was strange was that although his eyes were closed, he was holding a fishing rod in his arms, wearing a shoe on his left foot, while his right foot was bare, revealing a fair and slender foot. He looked like an immortal from folklore, devoid of any worldly aura.

Adam whispered in Timothy's ear, "Are we encountering an immortal?"

"Maybe," Timothy smiled, putting a finger to his lips and whispering, "Let's not disturb him."

Saying this, Timothy tiptoed forward and gently placed the shoe beside the white-clad man.

Just as he was about to turn and leave, he suddenly thought, what if the man kicked the shoe back into the river in his sleep? After some deliberation, Timothy decided to complete the good deed. He quietly approached and carefully put the shoe on the man's right foot.

"You're here."

A warm, clear voice sounded in his ear. Startled, Timothy looked up to see the white-clad man, who had been asleep, now wide awake and staring intently at him.

What do you mean by "you're here"? Timothy was baffled. He hesitated for a moment, then pointed to the shoe on the man's right foot. "Sir, your shoe fell into the river."

The white-clad man didn't respond, his eyes only scrutinizing Timothy's face closely.

Even someone as well-versed as Timothy felt uneasy being stared at so intently by such an ethereal person. He was about to avert his gaze when the man slightly nodded and said, "Thank you. My name is Austyn Powell. May I ask your name?"

"Timothy," he replied, glancing at the fishing rod in Austyn's arms. "Are you fishing?"

"Yes," Austyn nodded.

Timothy pointed to the empty hook. "But you don't even have bait. How can you catch fish?"

"Bait?" Austyn was momentarily taken aback before replying calmly, "Of course, I have bait."

"Where is it?" Timothy asked, puzzled.

Austyn pointed to the shoe on his right foot. "This is the bait."

Timothy blinked, dumbfounded for a moment, before realizing Austyn's implication. If the shoe was the bait, then the fish caught must be Timothy himself.

"What nonsense!"

Before Timothy could respond, Adam stepped forward, glaring at Austyn with a flushed face. "We kindly returned your shoe, and you insult us with such nonsense! I thought you were an immortal, but you're just a ruffian!" Adam grabbed Timothy's hand. "Alan, let's go. Ignore this crazy Taoist priest!"

Timothy was surprised. It was the first time he had seen Adam so impolite to a stranger. Moreover, he deliberately emphasized "we" to stress that the shoe wasn't found by Timothy alone.

"I meant no offense," Austyn said indifferently. He jumped lightly off the stone. "I am Austyn Powell. I have some knowledge of divination, medicine, and astrology. Three days ago, I divined that a noble person who can help me escape my plight would pass by here today. That's why I traveled here to wait."

"And this noble person... is me?" Timothy looked at Austyn half-believingly.

"Yes," Austyn nodded.

Timothy was speechless. He scrutinized Austyn, seeing his stern expression and serious demeanor, and didn't seem to be joking.

"Sir, forgive my skepticism," Timothy said awkwardly, "We don't know each other, and I have no idea how I could help you. If you were in my place, would you believe it?"

Austyn was silent for a moment before quietly saying, "No."

Timothy sighed in relief. "Exactly!"

"Belief is entirely up to Mr. Shaw. I don't force it," Austyn said, turning and walking away. After a few steps, he stopped and looked back at Timothy with icy eyes. "Before I leave, I want to remind Mr. Shaw of something... Within three days, you two will face a calamity of bloodshed. To avoid disaster, remember these eight words: 'The Dazzling Star enters the room, the year in quiet light.'"

Leaving these words, Austyn turned and left.

"The Dazzling Star enters the room, the year in quiet light."

After Austyn left, Timothy kept pondering the meaning of these eight words.

The Dazzling Star signifies disaster. The star entering something usually indicates trouble for a place or person. This was simple enough for Timothy to understand, but the latter part left him puzzled. Knowing nothing about astrology, he couldn't figure it out by thinking hard.

Adam's thoughts were simpler. He believed Austyn was just a fraudster. Talk of destiny and disaster relief was self-deception. So, Austyn's words were not worth taking to heart, and worrying about them was pointless.

Timothy thought Adam made sense. Considering the number of disasters he had faced, he had always managed to deal with them. Even if something went wrong one day, it would be fate. Rather than worrying about uncertain future events, he preferred to focus on the present and live each day well.

As for destiny and fortune, those are beyond our control. Everything should go with the flow. With this in mind, Timothy felt at ease.

Timothy wasn't a seer and couldn't predict the future. So, he treated his encounter with Austyn as a negligible episode, unaware of how this meeting would alter his fate.

But soon, the series of events that followed slapped him in the face.

Three days later, at noon, when Timothy and Adam stood in Mausoleum Rudolf, looking at the ruins burnt to ashes, cold sweat trickled down Timothy's back. Adam, who had once dismissed Austyn's words, was speechless.

This fire in Mausoleum Rudolf swept through almost the entire street, causing numerous casualties, especially at the inn where the fire started, resulting in the loss of thirty-six lives, with no survivors.

Timothy and Adam had originally intended to stay at that inn. If not for the heated argument Timothy had with the innkeeper the previous day, resulting in them being kicked out, they might have also been caught in the disaster.

As for why Timothy, usually so amiable, had a fierce argument with the innkeeper, it all began on the day Timothy and Adam arrived in Mausoleum Rudolf.

After a long and arduous journey, they reached the administrative center of Kamal, Mausoleum Rudolf. The city was bustling with people, and the citizens were flocking in one direction as if attending a market fair. Upon inquiry, they learned that Kamal had been plagued by frequent natural disasters recently. The people, who believed in the interaction between heaven and man, naturally attributed these calamities to the current ruler's loss of virtue, thinking that the heavens were punishing them for his misdeeds.

Consequently, rumors and unrest spread throughout the city. To calm the populace, the governor of Mausoleum Rudolf decided to hold a grand ritual to pray for good weather and peace.

As a passerby, Timothy initially had no interest in joining the crowd. But when he heard that the ritual would be held at a temple called Temple Kalpana, he was taken aback.

The Dazzling Star enters the room, the year in quiet light.

Coincidentally, Austyn's words also mentioned "quiet light." Could this be a coincidence? If not, might there be a connection between Temple Kalpana and the bloodshed disaster Austyn foretold?

Intrigued, Timothy decided to join the crowd to investigate further, persuading Adam to accompany him.

As soon as they entered Temple Kalpana, they saw from a distance a tall man standing in the center of the altar in front of the main hall. The man was handsome and dignified, dressed in a dark blue robe with gold trimmings, exuding a noble and stern aura. He held a piece of talisman paper in his left hand and a brush in his right, muttering something under his breath. The people in the temple, however, were all lying prostrate on the ground, reverently worshiping the man on the altar.

The man in black chanted for a while, then suddenly raised his hand and scattered the talisman paper into the air.

At that moment, a sudden gust of wind swept through, lifting sand and stones. The crowd raised their sleeves to shield their faces. Miraculously, the overcast sky was cleared by the sudden wind, and a ray of sunlight pierced through the thick clouds, shining like a holy light on the man in black.

When the wind subsided and the people looked up again, the sun was shining brightly in a clear blue sky.

Seeing this miraculous scene, the people prostrated on the ground shouted, "Mr. Brown is virtuous and blessed with longevity!" and knelt down in waves. Even Timothy, who had seen much in his life, had never witnessed such a divine ritual.

"Who is that man on the altar?" Adam asked Timothy curiously. "Why do they revere him so much?"

"I want to know too," Timothy replied, frowning. "I thought he was just a sorcerer hired by the officials, but it seems he is someone extraordinary."

Perhaps their murmuring was too loud, as a man dressed as a commoner turned to them, glaring as if they had committed a blasphemy. "Show some respect! That is Governor Jadyn Brown, Mr. Brown!"

Another man beside Adam added, "You must be outsiders, so it's not surprising you haven't heard of Mr. Brown. Not only is he our governor, but he is also skilled in Mystical Magic, proficient in medicine, and has benefited almost all the people of Mausoleum Rudolf. He can cure diseases and control the elements. Calling him a living god wouldn't be an exaggeration!"

"Jadyn..." Timothy muttered the name softly. He had imagined that the ritual would involve setting up an altar and hiring a sorcerer to perform some ceremonial dances and mutter incomprehensible incantations. He hadn't expected the governor himself to lead the ritual to pray for the people.

"This Jadyn doesn't seem like a bad person," Adam said thoughtfully, looking at the imposing figure on the altar.

Hearing this, Timothy couldn't help but widen his eyes in surprise. He could hardly believe these words came from the same Adam who had once said, "There's not a single good official."

Chapter Thirty-Two: Battle of Words

After the ceremony, Jadyn didn't leave immediately. Instead, he was escorted into the grand hall of Temple Kalpana by a group of admirers.

The hall was spacious, bright, and magnificent. In terms of grandeur, it even surpassed Temple Lrisa in the Great Alvah Palace. Jadyn took his seat on the pulpit, surrounded by a crowd of people eagerly awaiting his discourse. Timothy and Adam were among them.

"What's a discourse?" Adam asked curiously. "I've never heard of it before."

"It's when a bunch of high society folks get together to chat," Timothy whispered to Adam. "I've been to a few with the King of Nixie during Rickie's time. It's all about rubbing shoulders with the elite, chatting away while scratching each other's backs, and sometimes talking till dawn."

"What do they talk about? Anything specific?" Adam's eyes widened with interest.

"Everything under the sun, except politics and social issues," Timothy frowned, nodding towards the pulpit. "Anyway, you'll see for yourself."

"Mr. Brown, you always say that human nature is inherently good. But if that's the case, why is there so much evil in the world? Why do ordinary people have to suffer so much?" an elderly man with gray hair asked Jadyn.

"As Mencius said, human nature is good, just like water tends to flow downwards. When stimulated, it can flow upwards, just like water on a mountain. Is it the nature of water to do so? No, it's the circumstances," Jadyn replied calmly. "I don't deny the existence of evil in the world, but as the sage said, it's a result of circumstances, not our inherent nature. Even evil-doers, as long as they're willing to change, can attain enlightenment."

"But didn't that also say," a young man raised his hand, "I'd rather betray the world than let the world betray me?"

His words elicited laughter from the crowd. Beside him, a woman quickly covered his mouth and tapped his head, saying, "What do you know! Too much storytelling!"

Jadyn smiled faintly and asked, "Have you ever eaten green beans?"

"Yes," the young man nodded.

"Then tell me, if I plant green beans, what will grow?"

"Green beans, of course."

"Exactly." Jadyn nodded and said, "As the saying goes, as you sow, so shall you reap. Mencius said that every person has four virtues: benevolence, righteousness, propriety, and wisdom. These are the seeds inherent in each of us. Without these virtues, where would goodness come from?"

As his words fell, the hall erupted in applause, with everyone nodding in agreement, as if they had just heard the words of a sage.

Even Adam seemed enlightened, looking at Jadyn with admiration in his eyes. He murmured to himself, "Mr. Brown is not only talented but also knowledgeable. No wonder the people of Mausoleum Rudolf admire him so much."

Timothy, who never liked these intellectual discussions, felt a pang of annoyance seeing Adam's almost worshipful gaze towards Jadyn. For some reason, he felt even more irritated when he saw that, casually humming to himself.

"Why are you humming?" Adam looked at him puzzled.

"It's nothing. I just don't think it's that impressive," Timothy said dismissively. Then, spurred by Adam's words, he couldn't help but feel a surge of competitiveness. He grabbed Adam's hand and pulled him back.

"Why rush? Let's see what he's got," Timothy said calmly, looking up at Jadyn on the pulpit with a slight smile. "I bet once I start, Mr. Brown won't be able to get off that stage."

Jadyn noticed the commotion and calmly observed Timothy from head to toe. He saw Timothy dressed plainly in coarse cloth, quite inconspicuous if not for the disturbance. Yet, upon closer inspection, Jadyn found his features handsome, with a hint of recklessness in his eyes. When he stepped into the crowd, he exuded a sense of presence.

Jadyn raised an eyebrow. "May I ask your name, sir? And where do you hail from?"

"I'm Timothy," Timothy replied with a smile, not wanting to attract trouble by revealing his identity. "Just an insignificant passerby. I don't want to disrupt everyone's enjoyment, but this gentleman seemed very dissatisfied with what I said earlier, and he seemed eager for me to debate Mr. Brown."

Jadyn smiled faintly. "What insight do you have, Mr. Shaw?"

"I'm just a layman, not as well-versed as Mr. Brown in quoting scriptures. I simply want to ask Mr. Brown, if human nature is inherently good, how does this goodness turn into evil?" Timothy asked.

Jadyn answered calmly, "Whether it's planting melons or beans, they will experience wind and rain during their growth. Even a good seed, if not carefully nurtured, can grow into a twisted plant."

"Since we all grow in the same environment, under the same sunlight and rain, why do some people follow the rules while others commit heinous acts? If everyone is inherently good, then where does this external evil come from? Isn't it from ourselves?" Timothy challenged.

Jadyn was momentarily speechless, unsure of how to respond.

Timothy didn't give him a chance to think and continued, "The reason why sages tirelessly persuade people to do good is precisely because it is hard to be good. On the contrary, bad people commit evil without any teaching, they do it instinctively. Everyone, imagine if your loved ones were brutally murdered, and the killer said, 'It's not my fault, it's the world's fault.' Would you forgive him?"

As Timothy finished speaking, the atmosphere in the hall changed immediately. Everyone looked at each other and began to whisper, discussing in low voices.

At this moment, Jadyn also realized the difficulty of his opponent, his expression finally changed, and he said in a deep voice, "You also said that most people, no matter how much suffering they endure, can still follow the rules for a lifetime. If people were as perverse as you say, why are there so many good people in the world? Why are there so many good deeds? Do you think they have some ulterior motives too?"

Timothy remained unfazed and calmly responded, "The reason people do good is that if they indulge their nature, everyone would be selfish and evil, and the world would fall into decay. As the saying goes, no one is perfect. I never consider myself a saint. But if a person cannot even face their own inner evil, how do they have the right to preach to others to avoid evil and do good?"

This last statement had a powerful impact, causing Jadyn's face to turn pale instantly. He abruptly stood up, his face alternating between red and white, as if he wanted to refute something, his lips moved, but he couldn't utter a word. Finally, in a fit of anger, he flung his sleeves and said in a low voice, "I'm not feeling well, let's call it a day."

After casting a cold glance at Timothy, he hurriedly left.

Jadyn's departure caused an uproar in the hall, as everyone surged forward, surrounding Timothy and Adam, shouting insults.

"Who the hell do you think you are to talk to Mr. Brown like that!?"

"Mr. Brown's discussions are not something you can just interrupt. What are you trying to achieve!?"

Seeing a mob surrounding Timothy, someone even raised a fist and punched Timothy on the forehead. Adam shouted, "Stop!", quickly rushed forward, and stood in front of Timothy, pushing the attacker away.

"Do you have any sense of reason!? What did Alan say wrong!? You can't win the argument, so you resort to violence, and so many of you bully one person! Shame on you!"

"Adam, stop wasting words with them, let's escape!"

Timothy initially just wanted to show off in front of Adam, but instead, it led to an unexpected disaster. Seeing that a fight was imminent, Timothy also had no desire to continue, grabbed Adam, and broke through the crowd, running away.

Timothy never imagined that they would escape Temple Kalpana in such a disgraceful manner. He also didn't expect the seemingly kind and peaceful people to turn into wolves and tigers, relentlessly chasing Timothy and Adam for several streets. It wasn't until they climbed onto a rooftop to hide that they finally shook off their pursuers.

However, their bad luck didn't end there.

A rumor quickly spread in Mausoleum Rudolf about how Timothy publicly rebuked Jadyn at Temple Kalpana, which made Timothy famous—though not in a good way, but rather infamous.

As the night fell, the two, looking for lodging, entered an inn, only to be recognized by the people around. The innkeeper not only refused them lodging but also mocked Timothy and Adam. Timothy, using his eloquence, got into an argument with the innkeeper. Infuriated by Timothy's sharp words, the innkeeper called a group of thugs to beat them out with sticks.

These continuous misfortunes drove Timothy mad. He had never encountered such hysterical rudeness. As they were thrown out by the innkeeper, he couldn't help but shout, "You who can't distinguish right from wrong, only knowing to bully others, will surely face retribution one day!"

Despite the anger and cursing, if they couldn't find a place to stay, they would still end up sleeping on the streets. Fortunately, they later found an abandoned, desolate temple on the outskirts of the city, which barely served as a place to stay for the night.

Timothy harbored a deep resentment, the more he thought about it, the more he felt that Mausoleum Rudolf was filled with a strange air, with people seemingly bewitched and not thinking clearly. Thinking of this, he couldn't help but rant.

Compared to the indignant Timothy, Adam was much calmer. He seemed more concerned about Timothy's injuries than their predicament. As he patiently listened to Timothy's complaints, he ground some herbs he found nearby into a paste with a stone. "They're just a bunch of ignorant brutes, Alan, don't let them get to you." Adam carefully applied the herbal paste to Timothy's wounded forehead as he spoke.

Timothy raised an eyebrow, "And who was it that was singing praises about Mr. Brown earlier?"

"Did I... did I do that?" Adam pursed his lips and looked down, feeling guilty.

Timothy mimicked Adam's tone, saying admiringly, "Mr. Brown is amazing! Not only is he handsome, but he's also knowledgeable and well-traveled!"

Timothy's impression of Adam was spot on, making Adam's face turn bright red in embarrassment, wishing he could find a hole to crawl into. In his anxiety, he punched Timothy in the chest, "Stop it! It's so embarrassing!"

Timothy winced, clutching his chest and taking a sharp breath.

Adam immediately remembered that Timothy was still injured and quickly reached out to rub his chest, "I'm sorry, does it still hurt?"

"It's just a flesh wound." Timothy leaned against the wall, feeling the gentle movements of Adam's hand on his chest. His anger turned into a soft tenderness, "Adam, thank you."

Adam tilted his head, not understanding.

Timothy looked into Adam's bright, clear eyes in the darkness, "It's my fault for being impulsive, dragging you into this mess. There were so many people, and the situation was dangerous, but Adam stood up for me, facing them all. I'm really happy."

Seeing Timothy's serious expression, so different from his usual carefree demeanor, Adam felt uneasy, "I... I just did what I had to. We're brothers, naturally, we share hardships."

"Would you do the same for the other brothers from Sabra Village?" Timothy asked, looking into his eyes.

"Of course," Adam's face flushed, and he shifted his gaze, "Why are you asking these strange questions?"

Timothy touched his chest where Adam had rubbed, feeling his heart beating faster for no reason. He smiled slightly and whispered, "I don't know."

"What did you say?" Adam asked, startled.

"Nothing," Timothy replied lazily, yawning and turning over to close his eyes.

"Alan!?" Adam jumped up and grabbed Timothy's shoulder, shaking him, "Don't leave me hanging like this!"

Timothy kept his eyes closed, hearing Adam's anxious yet helpless tone behind him, a smile forming at the corners of his mouth in the darkness.

Chapter Thirty-Three: A Chance Encounter

Timothy could never have imagined that his angry words would come true so tragically. The inn that was perfectly fine yesterday was now reduced to charred ruins overnight.

"No way... I just said it offhandedly yesterday, and retribution came so quickly??" Timothy muttered to himself, standing in front of the inn that had been burnt to the ground.

Adam, hearing this, shivered with fear. He grabbed Timothy's hand uneasily, "Alan, don't talk nonsense! This is their fate, it has nothing to do with you!"

"I know..." Timothy's mood was complicated. He certainly didn't want to believe that his words had come true, but words should not be spoken carelessly, even in anger.

"He is the arsonist!"

Suddenly, a shout came from the crowd, and all eyes turned sharply towards Timothy and Adam.

"Yesterday, I saw them arguing fiercely with the innkeeper, and they were thrown out!"

"That's right! I can testify! They must have set the fire out of spite after being kicked out!"

"Don't let them escape!!"

More and more people stepped forward, identifying Timothy and Adam as the culprits behind the fire. Soon, the angry crowd surrounded them, their eyes burning with hatred, suspicion, and contempt. These emotions snowballed, overwhelming Timothy and Adam.

The fire had happened too coincidentally and mysteriously. Even the usually brave Adam showed fear and clutched Timothy's arm, "Alan, what should we do?"

Timothy held Adam's hand and said, "Don't be afraid. As long as we have a clear conscience, they won't dare do anything to us."

Although he tried to comfort Adam, Timothy himself was inwardly terrified. Just as he was at a loss, the sound of hooves approached, and a group of soldiers escorted a palanquin towards them.

"It's Mr. Brown! Mr. Brown is here!"

Someone in the crowd shouted, and the previously fierce people immediately made way, respectfully kneeling.

The palanquin stopped in front of Timothy and Adam, and the curtain was slowly lifted. A graceful, tall man stepped out, none other than the governor of Mausoleum Rudolf, Jadyn.

Jadyn had changed his attire today but still wore a luxurious robe. His complexion was noticeably better than the previous day. Seeing Jadyn, the people who accused Timothy all started to complain to him, identifying Timothy as the arsonist.

Jadyn, however, remained expressionless and walked slowly towards Timothy.

"What? Mr. Brown, are you planning to arrest us?" Timothy didn't kneel, meeting Jadyn's gaze boldly.

Jadyn stared at Timothy for a moment, then suddenly smiled.

"Mr. Shaw, you must be joking. How could I dare?"

Timothy was stunned, "What?"

Jadyn waved his sleeves and respectfully bowed to Timothy in public, saying loudly, "Yesterday, I was blind to the great person in front of me and did not recognize Mr. Shaw's presence in Mausoleum Rudolf. I apologize for any lack of courtesy."

Everyone present looked at each other in disbelief.

Timothy frowned, "How do you know who I am...?"

Before Timothy could refuse, Jadyn enthusiastically grabbed Timothy's hand, his eyes narrowing with delight, "Mr. Shaw, I have prepared a feast especially for you to welcome you and Mr. Adam. If you don't mind, please move to my residence, and we can talk while eating."

Jadyn's gesture silenced all those who doubted Timothy. With Jadyn vouching for him, no one dared to gossip behind Timothy's back. It seemed that in people's hearts, the true culprit of the fire was less important than Jadyn's words.

Thus, Timothy and Adam were carried back to Jadyn's mansion in a grand palanquin.

At the banquet, Jadyn first punished himself with three cups of wine to apologize for the insults and attacks Timothy and Adam suffered due to the Temple Kalpana debate. He also hoped that Timothy would stay in Mausoleum Rudolf for a few days so he could make amends as a host.

Timothy was naturally unwilling to stay. The events of the past two days had completely ruined his impression of Mausoleum Rudolf. More importantly, he didn't want to delay his return to Poiema because of trivial matters, so he repeatedly declined.

However, Jadyn misunderstood Timothy's reluctance, thinking it was an expression of displeasure towards him and Mausoleum Rudolf. Therefore, he became even more anxious, even kneeling in front of Timothy, promising to properly discipline the people of Mausoleum Rudolf and ensure that such incidents would not happen again, begging Timothy to forgive him for Queen Owen's sake.

Timothy had assumed that most literati, despite their pretentiousness, would have some degree of pride. Even though he was known as a favorite of Queen Owen, he was still a eunuch and generally not well-regarded by court officials. So, he never expected that Jadyn, who usually carried himself with such high regard, would kneel before him for the sake of his career.

As the saying goes, "A person who has no shame is invincible." Faced with Jadyn, who was willing to discard his dignity, Timothy had no choice but to agree to stay at Jadyn's residence for another five days after a long negotiation.

Shaw Mansion was large, and Timothy and Adam, as honored guests, were arranged in the main house of the west garden. At nightfall, with the lanterns lit and fireflies dancing, a melancholy flute melody added a unique elegance to the tranquil west garden.

With nothing to do, Timothy accompanied Adam for a walk around the west garden. Thinking about how they had been treated like rats the night before, forced to huddle in a shabby temple, and now being honored guests at the governor's mansion, Timothy felt that life was indeed full of surprises, never knowing what would happen next.

"It seems that Taoist priest was right," Adam said with a sense of wonder. "We really did encounter disaster within three days."

"Indeed, it turns out we should thank the innkeeper for kicking us out."

"If you ask me, we should thank Alan. If Alan hadn't rebuked Mr. Brown at Temple Kalpana, making us the target of public outrage, we wouldn't have escaped the disaster."

"Wait a minute, 'The fire star enters the room, the year is in quiet light'..." Timothy paused, thoughtfully, "Doesn't this mean that we would have perished in that fire but escaped because of the Temple Kalpana incident?"

Just as he finished speaking, the flute music in the silent night suddenly stopped, and a low chuckle came from nearby.

Timothy was startled and looked towards the sound, seeing a slender figure in white standing under the moonlight by the bridge, holding a bamboo flute, ethereal and otherworldly.

"Alan! Could that person be..." Adam exclaimed, pointing at the figure.

"Yes, it should be him." Although there was some distance, Timothy saw clearly under the bright moonlight that the man on the bridge was none other than the Taoist priest, Austyn, whom they had met by the stream.

"Mr. Shaw, we meet again." Austyn turned, his expression serene and distant.

Timothy was surprised, "Why are you here? Did you know Adam and I would come here today?"

"Mr. Shaw, you misunderstand. This time is really just a coincidence." Austyn's lips curled slightly, "To be honest, Jadyn is my senior brother, and I am currently staying here as his guest."

With that, Austyn walked forward and bowed to them, "Although I am a guest here, I would like to extend my hospitality to both of you. If you don't mind, please join me in the pavilion for a chat. I'm sure you have much to say to me."

Under the bright moon, the night grew darker. At Austyn's invitation, Timothy and Adam went to the pavilion by the pond, where the three of them sat around a table, enjoying the fragrance of the lotus brought by the breeze, drinking under the moon.

Timothy raised his cup, "Master Powell, this cup is from Adam and me. Thanks to your eight words, we were able to escape disaster."

Austyn replied calmly, "Being able to escape disaster is your own good fortune. There is no need to thank me."

Timothy drained his cup and said, "Master Powell, your predictions are truly remarkable. May I ask who your teacher is?"

"Austyn is from Jacintha. At the age of five, he and my senior brother Jadyn apprenticed under Heart-Guarding Master Carter of Mountain Wenhaver Temple," Austyn replied.

"Master Carter!?" Timothy was shocked. "Do you mean the Master Carter, known as the greatest fortune teller in Great Alvah?"

"Yes," Austyn nodded.

"Who is Master Carter?" Adam asked curiously, not understanding.

"You haven't heard of the greatest fortune teller in Great Alvah?" Timothy patiently explained to Adam. "He helped the founding emperor conquer the land, strategizing from thousands of miles away, and was known as the greatest military advisor in Great Alvah. After helping the emperor secure the throne, he retired to the mountains to seek immortality and never intervened in worldly affairs again."

"Such a remarkable person is Master Powell's teacher!?" Adam was increasingly amazed, looking at Austyn with wide eyes. "Is he still alive?"

Austyn shook his head, "My master passed away five years ago."

Timothy counted on his fingers and said, "He lived a long life. Master Powell, why didn't you mention this earlier? No wonder your predictions are so remarkable; you were taught by a master. I truly didn't recognize a great person. My apologies."

Austyn replied humbly, "Although I studied under my master for fifteen years, I am far from matching his talent and wisdom. I didn't mention him because I feared bringing shame to his name with my limited abilities."

"Can Master Powell control the weather like Mr. Brown?" Adam suddenly asked, remembering something.

"Control the weather?" Austyn was taken aback, then realized, "You mean the ritual at Temple Kalpana?"

Adam nodded, "Mr. Brown was amazing. We saw him with a piece of talisman paper and a pen, performing a few gestures on the altar, chanting a few incantations, and the cloudy sky cleared up immediately."

Austyn smiled faintly and sipped his wine, saying softly, "How could I compare to my senior brother?"

When Austyn said this, his eyelids drooped, and his long, thick eyelashes covered his eyes, as if he was hiding something unintentionally.

"But to us ordinary people, Master Powell is already very impressive. In contrast, I'm just a commoner. I can't even protect my own life, let alone save others. How can I change your fate and help you out of your predicament?" Timothy said.

"Actually... I can't explain it either." Austyn's eyes darkened as his gaze fell on the wine swirling in his cup.

"Even someone as wise as Master Powell has things they don't know?" Timothy asked.

Austyn smiled bitterly, "Austyn is not a god, just a mere mortal. In the grand scheme of things, Austyn is nothing but a tiny speck of dust. It's only natural to have mysteries that are beyond comprehension."

With that, Austyn stood up silently, walked to the balustrade, and looked up at the bright moon, his brows furrowed slightly, as if lost in thoughts only he knew.

Timothy and Adam exchanged glances, neither daring to speak, fearing they would disturb Austyn's contemplation.

After a long time, Austyn sighed softly and said, "Indeed, to outsiders, it may seem that Austyn, with his skills and a senior brother who holds high office, living in this peaceful and serene place, leading a life of comfort... Compared to those struggling to survive, Austyn should have no worries or concerns about fate."

Timothy didn't know why Austyn suddenly felt this way. It was as if Austyn was not answering Timothy's question but talking to another part of himself, using this self-dialogue to express some unresolvable emotions.

Perhaps Austyn had some unspeakable troubles. Even if Timothy could indeed change Austyn's fate, as Austyn claimed, they had only just met. Who could open their heart completely and without reservation to a stranger they had just met?

"Sorry. Austyn's old habit of talking to himself kicked in again." When Austyn turned back, his face was once again calm and smiling. "Tonight is a rare, beautiful night. Why talk about such disheartening things? Meeting friends over wine is a pleasure. It's rare for the three of us to come together like this, enjoying the moonlight and drinking. Austyn is already content, with no other desires."

Timothy picked up the wine jug, filled his cup to the brim, and walked over to Austyn. "Master Powell, let's drink this cup together."

Austyn took the cup from Timothy and drained it in one gulp.

Timothy gazed intently at Austyn and said seriously, "Even a chance meeting is a kind of fate. After drinking this cup, Austyn is my friend. From now on, no more formalities."

Austyn stared at Timothy, speechless.

"But since we are friends, it would be too formal to call you Master Powell," Timothy said with a bright smile. "From now on, we will address each other as brothers. Austyn, if you have any concerns, don't hide them. Feel free to talk to me."

"Ahem!" The atmosphere was just right when Adam's dry cough broke the silence.

"Of course, there's also Adam." Timothy nudged Adam and laughed, "After all, Austyn has saved our lives, right, Adam?"

Adam turned his head away, "I am unlearned and rustic. I don't dare to comment on Master Powell's personal affairs. But if anyone dares to disrespect Master Powell, I won't let them off."

Timothy, always perceptive, immediately sensed the hint of jealousy in Adam's words.

In the past, whether in Sabra Village or in Rickie, Adam always hid his feelings, never showing a trace. However, since he decided to follow Timothy back to Poiema, Adam seemed to have gradually opened up and now even showed a bit of jealousy towards Timothy.

Timothy was pleased by this change. He preferred the current Adam, who was a bit reserved but had his own thoughts, over the overly cautious Adam of the past.

He smiled and put his hand on Adam's shoulder, "Who are you talking about? Who dares to disrespect Austyn?"

"Whoever responds, that's who I'm talking about."

Their playful banter quickly lightened the heavy atmosphere. Austyn, though silent, watched their interactions with great interest. Perhaps influenced by Timothy and Adam, Austyn's lips also curved into a gentle smile, and the melancholy that had clouded his face dissipated without him noticing.

Chapter Thirty-Four: The Perverse Habit

Jadyn and Austyn's appearance completely disrupted Timothy's plans. Moreover, everything that had happened in Mausoleum Rudolf left Timothy utterly perplexed. For instance, he had no acquaintances in Mausoleum Rudolf and had never dealt with the authorities, so how did Jadyn know his identity? And what exactly were Austyn's unspoken troubles, and what did he mean by changing fate?

Thinking it over and over, Timothy decided to stop pondering. He was not like Austyn; fortune-telling and divination were not his strengths. Fortunately, five days passed in the blink of an eye, and instead of overthinking things, he decided to go with the flow, knowing that all mysteries would eventually be resolved.

Speaking of divination, a sudden thought struck Timothy. Since Austyn was so skilled in this area, why not have him help foresee his own—or rather, Christopher's future fate? This way, he could avoid misfortune and ensure smooth sailing.

Timothy thought about it and then directly asked Austyn. Of course, he didn't speak too plainly or reveal any details, only mentioning that he had a very important task to undertake.

However, Austyn did not answer directly. He just looked into Timothy's eyes and asked, "If I predict a bad outcome, are you planning to give up?"

"Uh..." Timothy was taken aback, "No, no matter what the result is, I will go through with it."

"Then that settles it," Austyn said with a faint smile, as if he had already anticipated Timothy's response. "The more important the matter, the less you should approach it with a mindset of taking shortcuts. Sometimes, success or failure doesn't depend on the odds but on whether you have a resolute determination. Without the determination to succeed, even the most meticulous planning can end in failure."

Austyn's words were enlightening, giving Timothy a sudden clarity, as if a fog had lifted.

"Austyn, you're right. It was foolish of me to ask," Timothy admitted, feeling a bit embarrassed and regretting his foolish question.

"However..." Austyn added, seemingly not wanting to disappoint Timothy, "if you're still worried, you can try getting a divination lot at Temple Kalpana."

"Temple Kalpana?" Timothy's eyes lit up with renewed hope. "Does this mean that Temple Kalpana is quite effective if even Austyn says so?"

Austyn, however, replied seriously, "It's just for peace of mind. Honestly, it doesn't matter where you go."

Pfft—Austyn's blunt truth doused Timothy's hope like a bucket of cold water, nearly making him stumble.

"Austyn, you're too honest! At times like these, shouldn't you say something comforting to cheer me up?" Timothy complained.

Austyn obligingly said, "Temple Kalpana is very effective—"

"That's so insincere! Too fake!!" Timothy shouted in frustration.

In the end, despite knowing it was merely for psychological comfort, Timothy obediently went to Temple Kalpana to get a divination lot.

Jadyn initially wanted to accompany him but was refused by Timothy. It wasn't that Timothy had anything against Jadyn; it was just that Jadyn attracted too much attention. Every time Timothy went out with him, they were surrounded by eager townsfolk, blocking the entire street and making it impossible for Timothy to move.

Seeing Timothy's insistence on going alone, Jadyn had no choice but to arrange for a sedan chair and assigned two highly skilled guards to follow Timothy, treating him like some rare treasure.

Timothy felt that Jadyn was overreacting a bit. However, considering his previous experiences in Mausoleum Rudolf, he realized that Jadyn's concern wasn't entirely unwarranted.

During these few days, Timothy gradually understood Jadyn's character. Jadyn had originally come from a declining local family in Jacintha and apprenticed under Master Carter, learning the arts of divination and medicine. After Master Carter's passing, he traveled with Austyn, meeting renowned figures and gaining recognition and recommendations through his skills and eloquence, eventually entering the bureaucratic world.

In Timothy's view, Jadyn was somewhat superficial and hypocritical but not as cunning as Penelope. His greatest wish seemed to be that Timothy would speak well of him to Queen Owen upon returning to Poiema.

In contrast, Austyn was much more detached, not as eager for official positions as his senior brother. Timothy believed that Austyn's knowledge was no less than that of his senior. Austyn was well-versed in a wide range of subjects, from astronomy and geography to state affairs and the lives of ordinary people, from the arts to the philosophies of various schools of thought, all of which he could discuss at length.

Although Timothy wasn't as learned as Austyn, he was very curious by nature and could always find something to say on any topic. Thus, the two of them never ran out of things to talk about.

Timothy's luck seemed to be turning when he drew an exceptionally favorable lot at Temple Kalpana.

Could this be a sign that he was about to turn his fortunes around? Timothy happily tucked the lot into his pocket, thinking he must share this good news with Austyn and ask for an interpretation. However, as he stepped out of Temple Kalpana, he bumped right into someone.

"Ouch..." Timothy rubbed his head where it had been hit and was about to speak when he heard the other person curse, "Who the hell can't watch where they're going!"

Timothy looked up, ready to retort, but both parties froze as their eyes met.

The person was a young man in his twenties, dressed in loose robes, tall and slender, with strikingly handsome features, looking familiar.

"Timothy!?" The man was the first to react, exclaiming in surprise, "What a small world! Do you remember me?"

Timothy's mind raced, and suddenly he had a flash of recognition, pointing at the man, "Urijah!?"

"So Jadyn knew my identity because of you!" Timothy downed his cup of wine and slammed it on the table.

In a refined pavilion nestled deep in a bamboo grove outside Temple Kalpana, Urijah and Timothy sat across from each other. Urijah, with a cautious smile, poured wine for Timothy.

"After all, in Mausoleum Rudolf, there are few who dare to confront Jadyn publicly. Timothy became the talk of the town overnight. As Mr. Brown's drinking buddy, I had to warn him, lest he unknowingly offend the Queen's favorite."

"You're quite the loyal friend," Timothy remarked, giving him a sidelong glance. "But I don't understand, you were serving the Queen well in the palace. What brings you here?"

"Well, it's my own fault," Urijah admitted with an awkward laugh and proceeded to recount how he had an affair behind

Queen Owen's back, leading to his expulsion from the palace when it was discovered.

Timothy was dumbfounded, "I don't know whether to call you brave or lucky."

Timothy had met Urijah in Terrace Torger. Even back then, Timothy knew Urijah was a wild spirit, driven by his lower instincts. But he hadn't expected Urijah to remain incorrigible even after entering the palace, daring to flirt under Queen Owen's nose. It was a miracle she hadn't executed him in a fit of rage.

"A person only lives once. If you can't indulge in pleasures, what's the difference between living and dying?" Urijah downed a bowl of wine and wiped his mouth, "Besides, the palace isn't a place you can easily get into. Wasting such an opportunity would be a disgrace to my good looks."

"Such twisted logic," Timothy retorted with an eye roll.

Though reluctant to admit it, there was some truth to Urijah's words, and Timothy found himself unable to argue.

"But..." Urijah suddenly changed the subject, "speaking of bravery, I'm nothing compared to someone here..."

Timothy was puzzled, frowning, "Someone?"

"Far away..." Urijah stood up with the wine jug, swaying as he walked behind Timothy and leaned close to his ear, "But also right in front of me."

Timothy felt paralyzed, his body stiffening as he struggled to calm himself. "What do you mean?"

Seeing Timothy's rigid posture, clearly struck by his words, Urijah became bolder, wrapping an arm around Timothy's neck.

"Timothy, I've already been kicked out of the palace, so why continue playing dumb with me?" Urijah chuckled softly, his voice low, "As Queen Owen's attendant, you secretly communicated with the emperor without anyone knowing. If I hadn't accidentally discovered the letter you sent to the emperor, if I hadn't overheard the emperor calling your name while pleasuring himself in Hall Zona, I wouldn't have believed it."

Urijah's voice buzzed in Timothy's ears, like the whisper of a demon.

Timothy downed his drink in one gulp, keeping a composed facade while his mind raced. If Queen Owen knew about his affair with Christopher, he would have already been executed, not sitting here casually drinking with Urijah. Clearly, Urijah hadn't reported him and Christopher to Queen Owen.

Realizing this, Timothy felt a bit more at ease. Even so, he couldn't hide his displeasure, and he spoke coldly, "What is it then? Are you trying to blackmail me? Extort me? Or do you want me to thank you for not betraying us to the Queen?"

"Nothing of the sort!" Urijah laughed heartily, "I have no power or influence now, but as long as I stick close to Mr. Brown, I won't lack for anything. Blackmail and extortion are meaningless to me. I just feel it's a pity."

"A pity for what?"

"Sigh, I, Urijah, have nearly slept with everyone in the harem, but the emperor, the biggest prize, slipped away from me just as I was about to have him."

"What did you say!?" Timothy's expression changed abruptly. He stood up swiftly, grabbing Urijah by the collar and shouting, "What did you do to the emperor!?"

Urijah, already somewhat drunk, seemed unaware of Timothy's simmering rage. He cheerfully recounted how he had intercepted Timothy's letter and used it to threaten Christopher. Just as Christopher was about to succumb, Arya had intervened, thwarting his plans.

The mystery that had long puzzled Timothy was finally unraveled. The reason he hadn't received any reply from Christopher was because Urijah had intercepted his letters and used them to blackmail Christopher.

Realizing that his own letter had nearly caused Christopher's downfall, Timothy's anger surged. "You beast!" Fueled by the alcohol, Timothy threw a punch, landing squarely on Urijah's face. Caught off guard, Urijah took the full brunt of the punch and fell back, seeing stars.

"You hit me...?" Urijah held his quickly swelling face, pouting in pain, and began to wail loudly, "What did I do to deserve this? Did I bully the emperor? Did I report you two?"

"Shut up!" Timothy grabbed Urijah by the collar again and slapped him several times, "You dared to threaten the emperor; you deserve this! You should be grateful I didn't bring a knife; otherwise, I'd stab you, you scoundrel!"

The secluded pavilion, often used by Urijah for his trysts, was perfect for privacy. Once the door was closed, no one outside would hear anything.

Blood streamed from Urijah's nose. He was the type to loaf around, his large frame mostly useless fat. He couldn't match Timothy's strength, so he lay on the ground, playing dead, wailing, "Go ahead, hit me. I, Urijah, am not afraid of death; why would I fear a beating?"

Seeing his shameless behavior, Timothy's anger flared. Clearly, physical punishment was ineffective on Urijah. So he stripped Urijah naked and had his men bring ropes to bind him tightly.

"Mr. Shaw... what are you doing..." The two guards were dumbfounded.

"He's shameless, so I'll treat him accordingly," Timothy said angrily, "Take him out and parade him through the streets!"

"Mr. Shaw, please don't be impulsive!" One of the guards quickly intervened, "Mr. Rogers is Mr. Brown's friend. If you parade him through the streets, how will Mr. Brown maintain his dignity? What will the people say?"

The other guard also advised, "Yes, Mr. Shaw, for Mr. Brown's sake, spare him this time."

Timothy considered this but was unwilling to let Urijah off easily. He grabbed the guard's whip and lashed Urijah fiercely. Urijah screamed like a slaughtered pig, his bound and naked body twitching.

Unsatisfied, Timothy continued lashing him.

Oddly, despite the pain, Urijah's moans began to mix with pleasure. The harsher Timothy lashed, the more Urijah seemed to enjoy it. When Timothy realized something was amiss, Urijah's member had already risen, swaying in the air with each lash.

Timothy had never seen such depravity. As the one administering the punishment, it now seemed he was giving Urijah some perverse pleasure. Urijah's stubborn erection, leaking fluid despite the beating, seemed to mock Timothy's efforts.

"How dare you!" Timothy, furious, grabbed Urijah's erect member and squeezed hard.

Urijah screamed and nearly passed out, his member twitching and ejaculating onto Timothy's hand.

"Bastard!" Timothy instinctively slapped Urijah, leaving another vivid handprint on his face.

Timothy never imagined Urijah had such a masochistic streak.

"Disgusting!" Timothy looked at his hand in disgust, feeling the sticky mess. He grabbed Urijah by the hair, dragging him over, and ordered, "Lick it clean! Lick off your own filth!"

"Yes..."

Under Timothy's domination, Urijah obediently extended his tongue, licking Timothy's palm and the back of his hand clean, like a dog begging for its master's favor.

Chapter Thirty-Five: Heartwarming Lotus Seed

Timothy hadn't returned all night, leaving Adam sleepless and worried.

That morning, before Timothy left, he mentioned going to Temple Kalpana to offer incense and seek divination. But if it was just to offer incense and seek divination, why hadn't he returned all night? Had something happened at Temple Kalpana? Or perhaps Timothy had encountered an ambush on his way? Mausoleum Rudolf wasn't friendly to them, and despite Jadyn's repeated assurances, there was still a chance that some hostile townsfolk might have caused trouble for Timothy.

But Timothy had left with two skilled guards. If someone had caused trouble, those guards wouldn't have stood idly by. If Timothy hadn't met with foul play, what other reason could there be? It couldn't be that he was lingering in a brothel, could it?

Compared to the former, the latter at least meant Timothy was safe. Others might comfort themselves with this thought, believing Timothy was fine. But Adam couldn't—wouldn't—accept the latter because it was a far greater blow to him psychologically than the former.

Adam grew more despondent, not just for Timothy but also for himself. Timothy wasn't his, nor did Timothy owe him any loyalty. So why was he, like a worried wife fearing her husband's infidelity, tossing and turning in anxiety and suspicion?

Adam lay awake with anxiety, finally falling into a shallow sleep as dawn broke.

In the early morning, half-awake, Adam was startled by a commotion. Thinking it was Timothy returning, he leapt out of bed, quickly dressed, and hurried to the front yard.

Jadyn stood with several guards in the courtyard, dressed formally, seemingly about to leave. His expression was serious as he gave urgent instructions. Amidst the exchange, Adam faintly heard the name "Mr. Shaw."

"Mr. Brown," Adam approached cautiously, worriedly asking, "Alan... Timothy didn't return all night. Is something wrong?"

"Mr. Shaw?" Jadyn smiled slightly. "I was just instructing my subordinates about this. Mr. Shaw met an old friend outside Temple Kalpana yesterday. They hadn't seen each other in a long time, so they drank heavily and couldn't walk afterward. Unfortunately, I have urgent matters to attend to and can't personally fetch him. I've sent more men to bring Mr. Shaw back."

Just drunk? Adam felt somewhat relieved and quickly said, "Mr. Brown, may I go with them? I'm worried he might cause trouble for everyone..."

Jadyn nodded with a smile, "Why not? With Mr. Garcia there, I can leave with peace of mind."

"Mr. Shaw and Mr. Rogers are on the second floor."

Adam followed the guards to a secluded pavilion deep in the bamboo grove outside Temple Kalpana. As they entered, the innkeeper greeted them enthusiastically and led them upstairs.

Mr. Rogers? Adam was puzzled. Timothy had an old friend in Mausoleum Rudolf? Why hadn't Timothy ever mentioned this? When the suspicious Adam reached the second-floor pavilion and opened the door, he was hit by a strange, pungent smell of alcohol, causing everyone to step back. The odor was not just from alcohol but was mixed with an indescribable stench, more intense than that of overnight fish guts.

Adam instinctively wrinkled his nose in disgust.

What had happened in this room? When Adam walked in and saw the scene, he froze like a block of wood, his mind going blank.

Wine jars were scattered, clothes thrown everywhere. Amidst the mess, Timothy lay on the ground, shirt open, one hand holding a soft whip, his head resting on another man's chest.

The man under Timothy was bound tightly, stark naked. Initially, Adam thought the man's fair skin was covered in red centipedes, but upon closer inspection, he saw they were lash marks.

The most shocking part was the man's abdomen and the floor beneath him, dotted with an unknown white fluid.

Both Timothy and the man were dead drunk, sleeping heavily, their faces flushed from the night's excesses.

For a moment, Adam was paralyzed, followed by a lightning bolt of realization that left him feeling as though he had fallen into an ice-cold pit. His limbs turned cold and trembled despite the rising sun.

He dared not imagine what had transpired in this room. No, it wasn't that he dared not but that he didn't want to. If this was a surreal nightmare, he wanted to wake up immediately.

"So noisy..."

The noise seemed to wake Timothy. He groggily opened his eyes, rubbed his aching head, and slowly focused on the people before him.

The guards quickly helped Timothy up.

"Mr. Shaw, are you alright?"

"You..." Timothy looked around in confusion, not understanding where these people had come from. When his focus finally landed on a familiar face, his muddled brain seemed to snap into clarity.

"Adam!?" Timothy was surprised to see him. "Why are you here...?"

Adam bit his lip, staring at Timothy, his eyes wide and filled with tears. Finally, he couldn't hold back any longer, and tears streamed down his face.

"You... you..." Adam's shoulders trembled as he took a deep breath, then shouted at Timothy with all his might, "You dirty old fox!"

With that, Adam burst into tears, turned, and ran out, storming down the stairs and out of the pavilion like a whirlwind.

"Adam!?" Timothy called out.

Adam ran with such determination and speed that Timothy, surrounded by guards, couldn't catch up. Timothy rushed to the window, looking out to see Adam running away, crying loudly, tears staining his sleeves, drawing the attention of curious onlookers.

"What's going on?" One guard peered out curiously.

"Don't you get it? It's love!" another guard said knowingly.

Embarrassed and ashamed, Timothy glared at them, and they immediately fell silent.

Timothy could feel that Adam's anger this time was unusual. In fact, it wasn't quite right to say that—Adam was always gentle, like a lamb, and rarely showed anger. Timothy couldn't recall a time Adam had ever been this angry in front of him. This time, Adam had been so enraged that he had used foul language, calling Timothy a "dirty old fox" in front of everyone. While Timothy accepted being called a fox, adding "dirty" and "old" hurt his pride so much that he wanted to kick the still-sleeping Urijah again.

By the time Timothy dressed and chased after Adam, he was long gone. Timothy questioned several passersby, but the trail went cold after a few miles, and he lost track of Adam.

Dejected, Timothy returned to the pavilion.

The culprit, Urijah, was already awake, dressed, and being escorted out by the guards. When he saw Timothy, Urijah's expression changed, and he coyly called out, "Timothy~" as he approached. Timothy couldn't stand his obsequiousness and grabbed his face, "You wretch! This is all your fault!"

"That's right, I, Urijah, am just Timothy's dog!"

Urijah's head was pushed back while his arms wrapped around Timothy's waist. Ever since last night, something snapped in his mind, and he became even more shameless and unruly than before.

Timothy, disgusted, shoved him away, lifted his long leg, and kicked him into the sedan chair.

"Timothy, don't leave me—" Urijah, unwilling to give up, lifted the curtain, his face a pitiful mess of tears, as if he intended to climb out.

"What are you standing around for!? Get moving! I don't want to see him again!" Timothy barked.

Under Timothy's urging, the bearers quickly lifted the sedan chair and carried Urijah away in a flash.

Adam, seemingly intent on punishing Timothy, disappeared for the entire day, his whereabouts unknown.

Timothy searched Mausoleum Rudolf for most of the day without success, and then a sudden downpour drenched him, leaving him soaked to the skin. Realizing that if Adam was deliberately avoiding him, further searching would be futile, he resignedly headed back.

Feeling frustrated and needing someone to talk to, Timothy naturally thought of Austyn.

Austyn lived in a quaint cottage named Clear River Residence, by the lotus pond in the western garden. This serene place, with peach blossoms in spring, lotus in summer, maple leaves in autumn, and plum blossoms in winter, was perfectly suited for someone like Austyn, who seemed to be otherworldly.

Austyn was writing diligently at his desk when he heard a knock on the door. Setting down his pen, he got up to open the door and found a bedraggled Timothy standing before him.

Without a word, Austyn ushered the soaked Timothy inside and handed him a towel. Timothy hurriedly thanked him, shaking himself like a wet dog and scattering water everywhere.

Outside, the torrential rain had begun to wane, leaving a misty haze over the water. Raindrops pattered on the lotus leaves, collecting in the center before forming into crystalline beads, much like the tears that had clung to Adam's eyes.

Timothy sighed deeply.

"Don't worry. Mr. Garcia is just upset. He'll come back once he cools down," Austyn said, approaching from the kitchen with a bowl of soup in his hands. "Here, I just made this lotus seed soup. Be careful, it's hot. You caught a chill in the rain, so this will warm you up."

"Thank you, Austyn." Timothy held the porcelain bowl in his hands, taking a cautious sip. He felt warmth spread through his body, "It's delicious! I can taste the ginger—it's very soothing."

Austyn said, "These lotus seeds are quite good too. Try one?"

Timothy scooped up some lotus seeds with his spoon and chewed thoughtfully. His eyes lit up, "These lotus seeds are so crisp and fresh, without any bitterness. They're perfect!"

Austyn smiled slightly, "I took a boat out this morning and gathered some lotus roots and pods from the middle of the pond. Then I shelled the seeds and made this soup."

Timothy was amazed. He had always thought that a refined gentleman like Austyn would be above kitchen work. He couldn't imagine Austyn not only cooking but also taking a boat out to the lotus leaves to gather pods, unconcerned about getting his hands dirty.

"Austyn, your future spouse will be very fortunate," Timothy said sincerely.

To his surprise, Austyn replied calmly, "I don't plan to marry."

"Why?" Timothy asked curiously. "Is this something you predicted?"

"Austyn doesn't like women," Austyn said, his clear eyes meeting Timothy's. "I only like men."

Timothy was taken aback, speechless.

Seeing Timothy's silence, Austyn asked, "Did I scare you?"

Timothy quickly shook his head, "No, no..."

I'm the same way, Timothy wanted to say, but felt it too revealing, so he swallowed the words.

"No wonder Austyn is still single, without a wife or children. A person as remarkable as you surely has many admirers."

"It's understandable that you're surprised. Anyone else in my position would probably settle down. But here I am, with my skills and a place to stay, yet I remain a guest at my senior brother's residence."

"True. Austyn, you said you followed your master at Mountain Wenhaver Temple. Mr. Brown stayed in Mausoleum Rudolf because of his official duties, but you have no such responsibilities and no interest in the bureaucracy. Why not stay at Mountain Wenhaver instead of living here?"

Austyn's brows furrowed slightly at Timothy's question. He gazed out the window silently. Timothy didn't push further, instead studying Austyn's profile—the high bridge of his nose, the sharp brows, and the soft red lips. There was a hint of indescribable melancholy in his delicate features.

The rain had stopped, and before he knew it, Timothy had been there for nearly an hour. Before leaving, he handed Austyn the divination lot he had drawn earlier.

After a rain, the weather turned chilly. Timothy shivered as he opened the door.

Seeing this, Austyn took down a cloak from the wall and draped it over Timothy's shoulders without a word. Timothy tried to decline, but Austyn simply said, "Don't move," and carefully fastened the cloak.

Their proximity made Timothy's heart beat faster for some reason.

Austyn was slightly shorter than Timothy, standing close enough that his eyes were level with Timothy's lips. Timothy noticed Austyn's hands, pale and slender with prominent knuckles, exuding an inexplicable allure.

Timothy thought of the lotus seed soup. Austyn reminded him of that soup—elegant but not aloof, pure but not fastidious, with a subtle warmth that was welcoming rather than distant.

After Austyn finished fastening the cloak, Timothy put on his hat and glanced at Austyn, who seemed to have something to say.

"You, tonight..." Austyn hesitated, "Can Austyn come to see you?"

Timothy guessed that Austyn might finally want to open up to him and said with a smile, "We're friends, remember? Friends don't need to be formal. Come find me anytime."

Austyn lifted his gaze, a hint of pain flickering in his eyes.

But the pain vanished so quickly that Timothy wondered if he had imagined it.

Austyn smiled warmly and nodded, "Alright, it's a deal."

Chapter Thirty-Six: The Most Unreliable Thing is the Human Heart

At night, Timothy lit the lamp and trimmed the wick, waiting for Austyn while bending over the desk, writing in bold strokes. After countless revisions, a missing person notice was finally completed.

It was a portrait of Adam, the result of his lifelong painting skills, with a line of large characters below: "A reward of ten taels of silver for information on the whereabouts of this person."

Timothy had battled with this missing person notice all night. By the latter half, he couldn't hold on any longer and fell into a deep sleep. When he woke up, it was already the next morning. He looked at the empty room and suddenly realized that he had been stood up by Austyn.

Austyn was not the kind of person who would break his promise. The reason he didn't come last night must be something happened, perhaps he was unwell or there was some other hidden reason.

Timothy first handed over his night's masterpiece to a servant, instructing them to copy a hundred or so and quickly post them on the streets.

Then he went to Qingchuan Residence.

Before reaching the door, Timothy saw Jadyn and Austyn standing by the pool, seemingly discussing something. Timothy was about to step forward and greet them when he heard a blunt remark.

"Unwell? You look quite spirited to me." Jadyn stared at Austyn, his attitude somewhat aggressive.

Austyn turned his head away, unintentionally avoiding Jadyn's gaze.

"Austyn." Jadyn's voice softened slightly, "Won't you even listen to your senior brother?"

Austyn's face was pale with a hint of weariness. He bit his lower lip, remaining silent.

Timothy walked quickly towards them and said loudly, "Mr. Brown, Austyn, what are you doing?"

Jadyn turned his head and, seeing it was Timothy, immediately put on a smile.

"Mr. Shaw, so you are here..."

Timothy walked up to them, looked at Austyn, then at Jadyn.

"What is going on? Quarreling first thing in the morning?"

Without knowing the full story, Timothy instinctively stood on Austyn's side and said to Jadyn, "Mr. Brown, Austyn is my friend. If you dare to bully him, I won't let you off."

Jadyn hurriedly smiled, "Mr. Shaw misunderstood. My junior brother and I have been friends since childhood, like brothers, how could I bully him?"

"That's best." Timothy turned to Austyn, "But Austyn, I have to say, I waited for you all night. What happened? Are you unwell?"

Jadyn also scolded Austyn, "Austyn, you were wrong to stand Mr. Shaw up."

Austyn bowed slightly, "I had a high fever last night and was bedridden, probably caught a cold while picking lotus roots at the pond during the day."

"High fever!?" Timothy was shocked and unabashedly stepped forward, pressing his forehead against Austyn's to check his temperature.

Austyn didn't expect Timothy to suddenly do this and blushed.

"Thankfully, it seems the fever has subsided?" Timothy murmured, releasing Austyn and breathing a sigh of relief, "I knew

Austyn wouldn't break his word easily; there must have been a good reason."

Austyn looked slightly ashamed, "You, I..."

Jadyn interrupted Austyn, smiling, "Austyn, see how much Mr. Shaw cares for you? He came here early in the morning to check on you. You should repay his kindness properly."

Timothy was confused, "What kindness? What repayment? My concern for Austyn is purely out of friendship, with no expectation of return. Mr. Brown, your words make it sound like I have ulterior motives. What do you mean?"

Jadyn laughed, "Nothing, nothing! Mr. Shaw is upright, and it's I who was rude. I shall not disturb you any longer and take my leave."

Watching Jadyn's departing figure, Timothy frowned, "Austyn, don't mind me asking, but does your senior brother always talk like that?"

"He's just like that, don't mind him," Austyn replied lightly, "No need to mention him. Has Mr. Garcia returned?"

"Speaking of which!" Timothy grabbed Austyn's hand, "Austyn, come with me, I have something to show you."

Timothy led a confused Austyn to the study, grabbed one of the copied missing person notices from a servant, examined it, nodded in satisfaction, and handed it to Austyn.

"Look at my masterpiece!"

Austyn took the notice, frowned at it for a while, and said, "You mean... the person in this portrait is Mr. Garcia?"

Timothy's eyes lit up, "You recognized him at first glance!? How is it? Didn't I capture his likeness perfectly?"

Austyn looked at the painting, then at Timothy, shocked by his work and unsure if he should honestly express his thoughts. He remembered Timothy previously complaining that he was too blunt and should sometimes say nice things to comfort others.

So he raised his head, using as much emotion as possible, and praised, "It's simply lifelike! Truly remarkable!"

"What a piece of trash!?"

Adam angrily tore down the posted notice and shredded it to pieces.

An old man beside Adam had been staring at the portrait for a long time. Seeing Adam suddenly tear it down, he said angrily, "Hey! Why are you tearing down the government's notice?"

Adam stomped on the shredded pieces, "This painting is hideous! It's offensive!"

"That's ten taels of silver!" the old man said, clutching his chest, "I don't recognize the man in the portrait, but they only want a lead. Why not make something up? Easy money!"

With that, the old man left, seemingly to find another notice.

Adam was speechless, not just at the old man's blatant intent to deceive the authorities, but also because he, the subject of the portrait, was standing right there, unnoticed. What use was this portrait as a missing person notice?

Adam was about to leave when he noticed a line of small characters on a fragment. He bent down, picked it up, and couldn't help but laugh.

The tiny characters read: "Alan is kneeling on the washboard. Adam, come back quickly."

Timothy, that guy, was he trying to annoy him or genuinely worried?

While Adam was staring at the small characters, a strange voice came from behind him.

"Excuse me, sir, may I disturb you?"

Adam turned abruptly. Before him stood a man, scruffy and about forty years old, with a gaunt face and a melancholic demeanor. But his clothes were of the finest silk, adorned with expensive jewelry, looking every bit like a wealthy merchant.

"Are you calling me?" Adam asked, puzzled.

The man nodded, "I saw you at Temple Kalpana, with that man named Timothy, the one who publicly refuted Jadyn, correct?"

Adam immediately became wary, thinking this man, like other townsfolk, was a follower of Jadyn and harbored ill intentions. He said sternly, "So what if I am? What do you want?"

The man respectfully bowed, "I have long admired you both. It's a great fortune to finally meet."

"You admire us?" Adam was taken aback, "Don't the people of Mausoleum Rudolf worship Jadyn as a deity? We opposed Jadyn, and they wished to tear us apart. How could you admire us?"

"Not everyone in Mausoleum Rudolf is a follower of Jadyn," the man said with a wry smile, "If you don't believe me, you can come to my house for a rest and hear my story."

The man turned and walked away. Only then did Adam notice that he was limping. The man didn't seem to care whether Adam would follow. His frail and stooped figure looked out of place amidst the bustling crowd.

Watching the weathered and faltering figure, Adam suddenly felt a surge of curiosity to understand what had happened to this man to make him so different. He quickly ran forward, supporting the man and said, "Sir, could you lead the way?"

The man's name was Dawsyn Clarke, a local of Mausoleum Rudolf. His home was in the western outskirts of Mausoleum Rudolf, nestled by the mountains and water, with dozens of acres of land. By rights, he was considered fairly wealthy. However, his estate was now sparsely populated, and there were very few tenant farmers left. In the height of summer, what should have been fields waving with wheat were instead overrun with wild grass, large swaths lying fallow.

Upon inquiry, Adam learned that Dawsyn once had more than a dozen tenant farmers, but now eight or nine out of ten had been taken by the authorities to serve as conscripts. The number of workers had suddenly decreased by more than half, making it difficult even for Dawsyn's family to make ends meet. In present-day Mausoleum Rudolf, or rather the whole of Kamal, tenant farmers had become a scarce resource. Landowners like him, with ample land but no labor to cultivate it, were everywhere.

But for Dawsyn, being undermined by the authorities was not the worst.

Dawsyn, now in his forties, had a wife named Patel. They were childhood sweethearts, deeply in love, and had been married for many years with two sons and a daughter, a family envied by their neighbors for their happiness.

The trouble began in the spring of two years ago when their youngest son suddenly contracted a mysterious illness. Dawsyn and his wife tried everything—they consulted doctors and performed rituals—but the child's condition did not improve.

As they watched their beloved youngest son weaken and approach death, a desperate Dawsyn thought of Jadyn. Jadyn's medical skills were well known in Mausoleum Rudolf; it was said that any illness cured by his hands would vanish completely. Desperate, Dawsyn and Patel took their son to Shaw Mansion to beg Jadyn for help.

Dawsyn was lucky; Jadyn agreed readily, but on the condition that they leave their son at Shaw Mansion and return in ten days. Jadyn never treated patients in front of outsiders. It was said this was one of his quirks or habits.

Dawsyn didn't mind. As long as his son could be cured, he would have waited not just ten days, but a whole month if necessary.

Ten days later, when Dawsyn and Patel returned to Shaw Mansion, they were astonished to find their son healthy and lively. Overwhelmed by Jadyn's miraculous skills, Dawsyn kowtowed repeatedly, while Patel, in tears of joy, clung to Jadyn's leg, calling him a benefactor.

Their son's recovery should have been a blessing. But unexpectedly, it became the catalyst for the couple's emotional breakdown.

Since their son's recovery, Patel seemed enchanted, running to town every day. She attended Jadyn's lectures or gathered with those who admired Jadyn, discussing the pursuit of immortality.

There were rumors that Jadyn was an immortal, practicing eternal life techniques. Patel firmly believed this, convinced that following Jadyn's teachings would make her immortal.

Dawsyn did not believe in such superstitions. This led to frequent arguments, with neither side able to convince the other. Dawsyn felt his wife had changed, even her way of thinking was different, and he often couldn't understand what she was thinking.

Patel stopped caring for the household and neglected their children, constantly talking about Mr. Brown, reciting scriptures and spells that Dawsyn couldn't understand, as if she had lost her mind.

Dawsyn knew that if this continued, he and Patel would eventually become estranged.

He tried to persuade her patiently, but by then, Patel was already stubbornly set in her beliefs, accusing Dawsyn of being heartless and unreasonable.

Despite Patel's increasingly extreme behavior, Dawsyn endured it for the sake of their long-standing relationship, until the day Patel tried to drown herself and their youngest son in the river.

That day, when Dawsyn and the servants dragged the drenched Patel and their son out of the river, Patel pointed at Dawsyn with resentment, saying, "Why did you stop me? We could have transcended together if not for you!"

Dawsyn was so enraged that he spat blood.

This incident crossed the line for Dawsyn. He could tolerate his wife's madness but could not allow anyone to harm their children, even if it was Patel.

After days of careful consideration, Dawsyn finally presented a divorce letter to his once-beloved wife. Patel was beyond saving, but at least this letter could protect their innocent children.

To his surprise, Patel showed no pain or sorrow. Instead, she looked relieved, as if grateful to be free from her husband's constraints, ready to follow her ideals.

Watching her resolute departure, Dawsyn felt a deep sense of desolation. In her eyes, decades of affection meant nothing compared to the illusory pursuit of immortality.

"What happened to your wife after she left the Clarke family? Did she achieve immortality?" Adam asked Dawsyn cautiously after hearing his story.

Dawsyn looked down in silence for a long time before squeezing out two words, "She died."

Adam was stunned into silence.

"As expected. How could there be such a thing as immortality in this world?" Dawsyn said with a bitter smile.

Adam remained silent, not daring to ask further, as it would be like rubbing salt into a wound, too cruel.

Initially, Adam thought Jadyn was just a capable charlatan, but now he realized Jadyn's influence was much more profound. Jadyn's methods seemed capable of drastically changing a person, turning a loving couple against each other and breaking apart a happy family.

The dead are gone, and the living grieve endlessly.

Patel's departure did not make life any easier for Dawsyn. Despite everything, Patel had been the love of his life. Decades of marriage ending like this left an irreparable scar on his heart.

Now over forty, Dawsyn should have been at an age where re-marriage and having more children were possible. But after Patel left, he aged rapidly, with greying temples and wrinkles beyond his years. He abandoned the thought of remarrying and focused on raising his three children, wanting only to live out the rest of his life in peace.

Dawsyn probably didn't want to share his painful past with any-one because, in Mausoleum Rudolf, few dared to oppose Jadyn. But Adam felt that there must be others with similar suffering. Most of them chose silence. So when outsiders like Timothy and Adam appeared in Mausoleum Rudolf, people like Dawsyn saw them as a rare opportunity to pour out their hardships.

As Dawsyn and Adam drank tea and chatted, they spoke of everything from Dawsyn's family and estate to Adam's back-ground.

Despite their nearly thirty-year age gap and different positions, they found an unexpected camaraderie.

From Dawsyn's words, Adam could tell he was a gentle father, unreservedly expressing his love for his children, which remind-ed Adam of his own father.

Adam often reminisced about his childhood, riding on his fa-ther's shoulders, holding a candied hawthorn, and visiting Tem-ple Fair with his brother. His father, though stern and quick to discipline with a broom, always took them out and conjured up treats.

After all this time, Adam had not had the chance to return to his hometown, Tim County, and he wondered if his parents were still alive. As he thought about it, Adam's eyes welled up. He re-alized that if his father were alive, he would be around Dawsyn's age. This realization made Adam feel a deeper connection to the frail, elderly man before him.

Chapter Thirty-Seven: Falling into the Mortal World

Adam visiting Dawsyn at his residence was something Timothy knew nothing about. Missing person notices were posted all over Mausoleum Rudolf, and many people came forward with so-called clues. Timothy, true to his word, generously gave each person who provided a lead ten taels of silver.

However, as time passed, Timothy's brows furrowed tighter and tighter. He wasn't worried about the money, as it was Jadyn's and not his own, so he didn't care about spending it. The problem was that despite the expenditure, reliable and useful clues were few and far between, and Adam was still nowhere to be found.

Timothy had never doubted his painting skills, especially since his masterpiece had been personally endorsed by Austyn. Timothy waited from morning until night, from the sun high in the sky to the moon hanging on the willow branches, but still had no success. If there was any gain, it was that a fruit merchant had specially sent him a large basket of fresh lychees, a rare and prized variety.

Timothy, being from the north, seldom had the chance to taste such delicacies from Lingnan. In a fit of frustration, he ate ten lychees in one go. Only when he felt his mouth dry and throat parched did he remember that lychees were warming and eating too many could cause a heat-related illness.

By then, it was too late. Although the weather wasn't that hot, Timothy was sweating profusely and urgently sought something to cool down and relieve his internal heat.

Suddenly, he thought of Austyn. Austyn was skilled in medicine and might have a good remedy for clearing heat and detoxifying the body. With this thought, Timothy went to Qingchuan Residence. Just as he was about to knock, the door creaked open, and there stood Austyn in a light, gauzy outfit.

At that moment, both were stunned. Austyn blinked and said, "You? I was just about to come find you..."

"Perfect timing! We were thinking the same thing; I was just about to come to you too," Timothy said, wiping the sweat from his forehead and swallowing, "Quick, help me cool down!"

"Cool down?"

Austyn hesitated for a moment, squinting as he looked Timothy up and down, suddenly realizing something.

"You... did you eat something you shouldn't have?"

"Ah, it's my greediness. How could I eat so many of those things at once?" Timothy lamented, pounding his chest.

Austyn understood. He lowered his eyes and said softly, "Why did you... think of me at this time?"

"Isn't it obvious? Who else could help me but you?" Timothy extended his hands and grabbed Austyn's shoulders, "Austyn, stop talking. If you don't help soon, I'll..."

Suddenly, a rush of blood surged to his head, and Timothy was really afraid he would start a nosebleed in front of Austyn. "If you don't help soon, it'll come out. Austyn, hurry!"

"It'll come out!?" Austyn was startled, his eyes instinctively shifting downward to look at Timothy's crotch.

Strangely, there was nothing unusual there. But Austyn didn't have time to think. As he reached out to support Timothy, their skin made contact, and Austyn was surprised. Timothy's body temperature was indeed higher than usual. Clearly, those lychees had quite an effect.

Austyn helped Timothy to his bedroom and sat him on the bed.

"Austyn? Why did you bring me here?" Timothy was puzzled, thinking he had only come to ask for a remedy to clear the heat, not to enter Austyn's bedroom.

Austyn blushed and said, "You really want to do this outside?"

"Outside, inside, I don't care. As long as it cools me down, anywhere is fine."

"I can't do it outside." Austyn seemed to reach his limit, turning his head, "You might not care, but I do."

With that, Austyn waved his hand, extinguishing the candlelight, plunging the room into darkness.

"Austyn??" Timothy was thoroughly confused by Austyn's actions. Before he could react, someone silently approached him in the dark, and a hand covered his eyes. Just as Timothy was about to speak, a soft touch landed gently on his cheek.

Timothy's chest jolted, his mind went blank.

It was Austyn's lips, with a slight, cool touch, gently exploring like a dragonfly on water, moving down from Timothy's cheek until they lightly captured Timothy's lips.

Austyn's kiss was reserved and controlled, hesitant to act rashly, as if Timothy were a fragile porcelain that might shatter. He simply pressed his lips to Timothy's, savoring or enjoying the moment, lingering there for a long time, unwilling to part.

Timothy's mind remained blank, feeling as if he were floating in the clouds, light and airy, on the verge of ascending.

Austyn kissed Timothy for a long while. When he finally released Timothy, Timothy's eyes had adjusted to the dark. He saw Austyn with lowered lashes, the hazy moonlight casting a delicate veil over him. Austyn had always been beautiful; Timothy had thought so when they first met, feeling that this man was untainted by the world, with an innate aura of purity. But now, standing shyly in the dim light, he seemed like a celestial being touched by the mortal realm, adding a touch of approachable humanity.

"Austyn, you..." Timothy suddenly felt awkward, his thirst now worse than before.

He had only come to Austyn for a remedy to clear the heat. Why did Austyn suddenly kiss him? What was happening?

Austyn's next action surprised Timothy even more. Austyn's slender fingers moved down to his waist, pulling at one end of his sash, and with a swoosh, the sash fell to the ground. Then came the outer garment, the robe, one piece after another, sliding off his body to his feet.

Austyn was wearing little to begin with, so undressing took no time. As he removed the last layer, revealing his smooth, fair chest, Timothy could no longer sit still. He stood up and grabbed Austyn's hand.

"Austyn! What are you doing? Why are you undressing?" Timothy asked, blushing.

Austyn looked down and said softly, "How else can I help you cool down?"

Timothy was completely stunned. Before he could react, Austyn's delicate body leaned into his embrace, a hint of shyness in his voice, "I have no experience, so please forgive me if I don't do well."

"Wait, wait!" Timothy quickly grabbed his shoulders, looking into Austyn's eyes, "Austyn, you've misunderstood. I... I didn't mean to do that with you! I just... just ate too many lychees and got overheated! I came to ask for a remedy to clear the heat!"

"Lychees...?" Austyn stared at Timothy, seemingly unable to understand what he was saying.

After a moment, Austyn finally understood. His face turned from red to white, then to an ashen color.

Timothy felt so embarrassed he wanted to crawl into a hole. On reflection, it was indeed his fault. Barging into Qingchuan Residence late at night, sweating and parched, speaking urgently without clarity—anyone would misunderstand his intentions.

Austyn had meant well, even agreeing to such an outrageous request. Now, with Austyn nearly undressed, Timothy only then explained it was a misunderstanding. Even the most patient person would be angry in this situation.

Timothy was deeply ashamed. He apologized repeatedly, leaving Austyn standing there as he bolted for the door.

It was too humiliating. Though he felt sorry for Austyn, Timothy couldn't bear to stay any longer.

The embarrassment was secondary; the main issue was Austyn's alluring physique. If he stayed alone with Austyn any longer, he feared he wouldn't be able to control himself.

As Timothy rushed towards the door, a voice suddenly stopped him.

"Timothy!"

Turning around, he saw Austyn still standing there, clothes disheveled, head bowed, gripping his robe tightly, knuckles white.

The moonlight cast a cool glow on Austyn's face, and Timothy noticed a faint tear streak on his cheek.

Had he made Austyn cry? Guilt surged through Timothy, making him feel helpless. "I'm sorry, Austyn, I didn't mean to tease you. I just..."

"I'm cold," Austyn softly interrupted him, his fingers gently caressing his bare skin. Timothy couldn't help but feel that the motion was particularly... enticing.

"You're wearing so little, of course you're cold," Timothy said, swallowing hard.

"Hold me, and I won't be cold," Austyn said, looking at Timothy with a gaze that sparkled with emotion.

It was an impossible request to refuse. After all, Timothy had come seeking Austyn's help first, and to refuse him now would seem heartless. Timothy extended his arms and gently held Austyn in his embrace.

"Who knew Austyn could be so charming?" Timothy said, trying to laugh off the situation.

"Of course I can be charming, but only to certain people," Austyn said, wrapping his arms around Timothy's waist.

With a rush of emotions, Timothy felt as if he were a firework being set off. What was going on with Austyn tonight? If the previous misunderstanding could be explained, then what was Austyn doing now, throwing himself into Timothy's arms?

A sudden realization struck Timothy. Austyn had mentioned he liked men.

Could it be that Austyn had feelings for him?

A gust of wind rustled the shadows of the trees outside the window. At that moment, Timothy noticed a dark figure standing by the window.

Someone was outside!

The shadow stood motionless, making no sound. Suspicious, Timothy tried to get a better look but was pulled back by Austyn, who then tumbled onto the bed with Timothy.

Austyn turned over, pressing Timothy down. Timothy frantically signaled to Austyn with his eyes, but Austyn ignored his desperate hints, silently tracing Timothy's features with the back of his hand.

Then, Austyn did something Timothy couldn't understand—he untied the ribbon from his hair, letting it fall like a waterfall, and then used the ribbon to cover Timothy's eyes. The fabric was so thin that even with his eyes covered, Timothy could still make out vague shapes.

"You..." Austyn whispered, "I'm sorry."

Before Timothy could respond, Austyn leaned down and began placing delicate kisses on his cheeks, neck, and collarbone. At the same time, his fingers gently undid Timothy's clothes.

Oddly enough, Austyn used no force, yet Timothy found himself unable to resist. Perhaps it was because Austyn's touch was so careful and tender that Timothy felt like a sacrificial offering to a deity.

Lost in thought, Timothy's clothes were gradually opened or removed. Though he couldn't see clearly, he knew Austyn's lips were still moving downward, first teasing his nipples, then tracing down his abs to his thighs.

Timothy's manhood lay dormant in its nest of hair, unaffected so far. Austyn hesitated for a moment before leaning down, his lips lightly brushing against the soft flesh. Timothy couldn't see him but felt like a kitten was playfully licking him. The tickling, tingling sensation gradually made him harden, and his breathing grew erratic.

"Austyn, that's enough..."

For someone as experienced as Timothy, he should have been accustomed to intimacy. But he felt a strong sense of guilt, fearing he would defile Austyn. So when things felt wrong, his first reaction was to push Austyn away.

But Austyn didn't retreat; instead, he took Timothy's manhood into his mouth, causing Timothy to shudder, his fingers tangling in Austyn's hair, wanting to grasp something but finding nothing.

Austyn was patient, moving his head up and down, taking Timothy deep into his throat and then pulling back until only the tip remained.

Timothy couldn't withstand such meticulous attention for long. Within moments, his erection stood firm, the head swelling.

Seeing Timothy's reaction, Austyn became more enthusiastic. He knelt between Timothy's legs, his head bobbing diligently, his lips making sucking noises. Perhaps finding a strand of hair bothersome, he tucked it behind his ear, revealing a delicate pink ear tip.

Timothy couldn't see this; he could only hear the sounds and imagine the scene. The unknown made it more tantalizing, and soon Timothy felt he might lose control.

"I'm going to come!" Timothy warned, pushing Austyn away.

But it was too late. Austyn didn't dodge, and Timothy's seed spurted onto his face.

Austyn didn't flinch. He leaned down again, taking Timothy back into his mouth, swallowing the remaining essence.

Chapter Thirty-Eight: The Beastly Nature of Man

When Austyn lifted his head from Timothy's groin, he choked and coughed a few times, covering his mouth.

"Austyn, are you okay?" Timothy sat up, and the fabric covering his eyes slid off.

Austyn's face was a mixture of pallor and a flush of arousal. His temples, eyebrows, and nose still had traces of sticky whiteness. Shocked and ashamed, he covered his face and turned away, not expecting Timothy to sit up and see him in such a disheveled state.

"Don't look!" Austyn's body trembled with shame, his thin chest rising and falling rapidly.

"Why?" Seeing Austyn like this, Timothy suddenly felt an inexplicable pang of heartache.

"You find me disgusting, don't you?" Austyn asked, his back still to Timothy, tears falling onto his pale fingers.

This was too strange. Austyn had initiated everything, but Timothy felt this wasn't what Austyn truly wanted.

"I'm sorry," Austyn said, his voice trembling. "I don't deserve your trust, nor do I deserve to be your friend."

Timothy's chest tightened. He grabbed Austyn's shoulders and turned him around, looking into his tear-filled eyes. "Austyn, listen to me. I never found you disgusting. But if you have something on your mind and keep it from me, that's when I'll be truly angry."

Austyn seemed lifeless, tears still streaming down his face.

"Still not willing to tell the truth?" Timothy asked, staring into his eyes.

Austyn kept his lips tightly shut, and Timothy, feeling a surge of determination, pushed Austyn onto the bed and bit down on his stubborn lips.

"If you won't tell me, don't blame me for being rough."

With that, Timothy kissed Austyn fiercely, prying his lips open and pushing his blood-tasting tongue inside, capturing Austyn's timid tongue.

"Mmm...!!"

Austyn panicked. Compared to his gentle kisses, Timothy's were wild and primal, like a storm overwhelming him. No matter how he struggled or pushed, Timothy always found a way in. In this clash of tongues, Austyn's initial composure was torn apart by Timothy's domineering assault.

With nowhere left to retreat, Austyn, inexperienced, felt like a child before Timothy. All his rationality and restraint crumbled under Timothy's aggressive kiss.

For the first time, Timothy felt he was seeing the real Austyn, not the calm and reserved version. Austyn was capable of chaos, struggle, shyness, and passion—an ordinary, emotional person.

When their lips finally parted, Austyn was exhausted, his limbs limp, eyes dazed. Even his groin was reacting, wetting the bed beneath him.

Seeing this, Timothy said softly, "Wait, I'll make you tell me."

He then lowered his head, taking Austyn's slender member into his mouth. Austyn's body shuddered, a high-pitched moan escaping his lips.

"No! Please, don't..."

Austyn pushed with all his might, his body twisting, but Timothy ignored his struggles. Instead, he sucked harder, his tongue teasing Austyn's most sensitive spot.

Austyn's limbs went numb, his resistance weakening until he had no strength left. Only his pale toes twitched in the air, his belly trembling as he released into Timothy's mouth. The speed was faster than when Timothy had climaxed.

Austyn stared blankly at the ceiling, feeling as if Timothy had not only taken his seed but also his soul.

Timothy swallowed Austyn's essence, licking him clean before rising and lightly kissing Austyn's lips.

"Well? If you don't talk, I'll continue."

"No... I'll talk..." Austyn said weakly.

Night had fallen, and the wind was cold. Seeing Austyn nearly naked, Timothy moved to light a candle but was stopped by Austyn.

"Just stay like this and listen to me."

"Alright." Timothy returned to Austyn's side, sitting cross-legged on the bed, looking at him quietly.

Austyn remained silent for a long time, long enough that Timothy wondered if he had fallen asleep. Finally, Austyn spoke in a barely audible voice, "Do you have any siblings?"

Timothy was surprised, not expecting such a question. "No, I'm an only child. Why?"

"I'm the same. I come from a humble family, with several older sisters. I'm the youngest."

"Your parents must have really wanted a son."

"Yes. Though my family was poor, my father was very strict with me. At five, I was sent to Mountain Wenhaver to study under Master Carter."

"You must have been homesick. A five-year-old child leaving his parents would cry a lot."

"Perhaps I did," Austyn said with a bitter smile. "But I was so young. My master said I was quiet, not crying or fussing when I left my parents. I would secretly cry at night. He thought I was unusually mature for my age. But I don't remember much of that. From what I can recall, my only family were my master, Master Carter, and my senior brother, Jadyn."

"So Master Carter was like a father to you, and Jadyn like a brother?"

"Yes," Austyn said, his eyes showing a hint of nostalgia. "Though I had biological parents, I received little affection from them. My master and senior brother were closer to me than family. My master was a free spirit who loved to take us on adventures, exploring the world's mysteries. We lay on the grass counting stars, crossed deserts to find ancient ruins, and spent sleepless nights solving puzzles he set for us. We even argued passionately over whether the chicken or the egg came first."

Timothy listened with envy. "That sounds amazing. I wish I could have lived like that."

Austyn turned to Timothy. "Since the moment I met you, I've had an inexplicable feeling about you."

"What kind of feeling?" Timothy asked, curious.

"That we're kindred spirits," Austyn said, adjusting his robe. "I just felt it."

Seeing Austyn shiver, Timothy took his hand and said, "If we're kindred spirits, why the distance? If you're cold, come closer." He patted his chest. "It's warm here."

Austyn blushed and leaned into Timothy's embrace. "That reminds me of my senior brother."

"Jadyn?" Timothy was surprised.

"When we traveled, we often slept under the stars. When it got cold, he would hold me like this, patting my back to lull me to sleep."

Timothy felt an inexplicable surge of jealousy. First Adam, now Austyn. Jadyn seemed to always make him feel envious without doing anything. "Seems like your senior brother treated you well."

Austyn noticed Timothy's tone and laughed. "My senior brother held me to sleep only before I turned eight. After that, he never did it again."

Timothy felt better but still tried to save face. "Why are you explaining so much? Do I look jealous of Jadyn?"

Austyn smiled slightly, refraining from banter, and continued, "In short, the first ten years after becoming an apprentice were the happiest, most carefree times of my life."

At this point, his eyes dimmed, the light in them replaced by a deep sorrow.

"Ten years... So something happened after you turned fifteen?" Timothy asked.

"Perhaps it was the years of wandering and harsh conditions that weakened my master's body. He was getting old and could no longer endure such strain. After I turned fifteen, we stopped traveling and returned to Mountain Wenhaver. Knowing his time was short, Master wanted to pass on all his knowledge to my senior brother and me. From then on, I took care of him while immersing myself in studies."

"Mountain Wenhaver, though I haven't been there, must be a serene and beautiful place, considering it's your master's retreat. Isn't it wonderful to study in such a place? What could go wrong?"

Austyn lowered his gaze. "The problem arose over who, between my senior brother and me, was more deserving of inheriting our master's legacy."

"Why? Weren't you both Master Carter's disciples? Couldn't both of you inherit? Why must it be one or the other?"

"I don't know. Master had his reasons, and it wasn't for us to question. I only cared about my interests, and as long as I could focus on my studies, it didn't matter who inherited. So, no matter what Master decided, I would have no complaints. But..."

Austyn sighed deeply, closing his eyes.

"Let me guess, Master chose you, right?" Timothy looked at Austyn.

Austyn opened his eyes, a bitter smile on his lips. "You saw right through me. How did you know?"

"It's simple, really. I deduced it." Timothy gently hugged Austyn from behind. "You're indifferent to fame and fortune, uncompetitive by nature. If Master had chosen your senior brother, you wouldn't have been upset. Everything would have been fine, right? If that were the case, you wouldn't be here frowning and sighing. So, Master must have chosen you, not Jadyn. And you, who regard Jadyn as an elder brother, feel guilty about it, right?"

"Exactly." Austyn nodded, sighing again. "Honestly, as you said, I wish Master hadn't chosen me. If he hadn't, maybe things would be different now..."

"Ah, I thought it was something serious! Is that all?" Timothy laughed. "Austyn, I have to tell you, just because Jadyn is your senior brother doesn't mean you have to let him have everything. Is he your parent? Your savior? Do you owe him a debt? If something is meant to be yours, accept it gracefully. You've done nothing wrong, so why feel guilty?"

Austyn shook his head. "No, it's not that simple between my senior brother and me."

Timothy frowned. "What do you mean? Is there more between you two?"

"In the matter of inheriting our master's legacy, my senior brother didn't complain, at least not outwardly. After Master's death, I began to miss our times traveling together and told my senior brother. He agreed, and we decided to travel again, just the two of us."

"Oh..." Timothy shrugged. "That sounds great. Even though your master passed away, you still had your senior brother."

"That's what I thought. We traveled, sharing our accumulated knowledge with the people, lecturing wherever we went. We welcomed everyone, regardless of their background, as long as they were interested."

Timothy admired him, eyes wide. "That's wonderful! Most common folk never get the chance to learn. You must have had many attendees."

"We did, sometimes too many to count. We usually lectured in temples and didn't charge, but we received donations, which we used for travel expenses and gave the rest to the temples. Our reputation grew, and even nobles and officials began to notice us. After each lecture, some prominent figures would approach us, offering to recommend us to the government."

"That's a great opportunity for a government position. But..." Timothy's tone shifted, "You had no interest in such things, right?"

Austyn nodded. "Indeed, I found academic pursuits far more appealing than a government career. I just wanted to travel and lecture with my senior brother. But... I later realized my senior brother didn't feel the same."

Timothy began to understand. "It's clear now. As you two gained recognition, nobles saw you as promising candidates for government roles. You weren't interested, but your senior brother was."

"Exactly. Jadyn craved fame and power. Despite being our master's disciples, our goals were different. Perhaps that's why Master chose me over him—because he saw that Jadyn didn't share our values."

"Then the solution is simple. If your senior brother wants to pursue a career, let him. You can continue your scholarly pursuits."

Austyn's eyes darkened. "I thought about that, but he wouldn't let me go."

"Why? You're not a child. You have your own legs. How could he stop you?"

Austyn's expression turned pained. After a long silence, he took a deep breath and spoke the hardest truth. "Because it was me, as Master Carter's heir, that the nobles were interested in, not him."

Timothy understood. It made sense. Being the heir to Great Alvah's foremost strategist, Master Carter, was a prestigious title. The nobles wanted Austyn, not Jadyn.

"But that doesn't add up..." Timothy mused. "At Temple Kalpana, I saw Jadyn's influence. People said he had great medical skills and had helped many. His abilities shouldn't be lacking."

Austyn gave a dry laugh. "Those deeds were actually done by me."

"What?" Timothy was stunned. "Wait, what about the sacrificial ceremony at Temple Kalpana?"

"I calculated the auspicious time for him in advance."

"And healing the people??"

"My senior brother never performed medicine in front of others. Instead, he brought patients to the mansion, and under the cover of night, he would bring me to their bedside where I would diagnose and prescribe treatments."

Timothy was left speechless. What Austyn revealed was beyond his comprehension. He needed all his mental faculties to process these revelations.

Previously, Austyn had hinted at this in their conversations. Timothy hadn't understood why Austyn, despite having no interest in officialdom, stayed at Jadyn's mansion as a retainer.

"So... you've been staying by Jadyn's side just to be his shadow, while he uses you as a tool to advance his career, deceiving the people!" Timothy leapt from the bed, grabbing Austyn's shoulders. "Why? Why didn't you just leave? Why degrade yourself for him? Was it all because of that so-called guilt?"

Austyn's eyes reddened, his face ashen. "I thought about leaving, but every time I mentioned it, my senior brother would beg me to stay, pleading for the sake of the people of Mausoleum Rudolf. He said that without me, who would save them?"

"You're not a savior! Why should the people of Mausoleum Rudolf rely on you? Jadyn is manipulating your conscience with innocent lives, forcing you to comply!"

Timothy's anger grew. He knew shouting at Austyn was useless, but he couldn't help it. If he didn't let it out, he felt he might explode.

"I know, I know. But I just can't bear to refuse him." Austyn looked up, tears streaming down his face. "He's my senior brother, my closest family!"

Timothy felt a lump in his throat, unable to speak.

"The one who can't leave isn't him." Austyn pressed his forehead against Timothy's chest, clutching his shirt desperately. His voice, choked with tears, seemed to come from deep within his throat. "It's me..."

Chapter Thirty-Nine: Plotting

Timothy was momentarily at a loss for words. As Austyn mentioned, Timothy, who had no siblings and whose family was safe and sound, indeed couldn't understand Austyn's obsession with his elder brother. Any comfort he offered would only seem like insincere pity and sympathy. All he could do was reach out and silently embrace Austyn, hoping to alleviate some of his pain and grievances.

At the same time, he took the opportunity to sort out his chaotic thoughts.

It was only at this moment that he finally understood the predicament and fate Austyn had spoken of when they first met. He also comprehended why Austyn had been so reticent the night they arrived at Shaw Mansion. Coupled with Austyn's unusual behavior tonight, a chilling thought crept into his mind.

"Could it be that everything you've done tonight... was also Jadyn's order?"

Austyn seemed unable to look Timothy in the eye and lowered his head deeply. After a long struggle, he finally nodded lightly while still in Timothy's embrace.

"Why?" Timothy felt a surge of anger rising again, "It can't be just to please me, right?"

Austyn shook his head, "You could say that, but... it's not that simple."

Timothy was puzzled, "What do you mean by that?"

"Do you remember the day you went to Temple Kalpana to get a divination?"

"Of course, I remember. I gave the divination slip to you... Oh, right, you haven't interpreted it for me yet."

"That night, I had already interpreted it. I was just about to find you when my brother came. He knew you had gotten a divination at Temple Kalpana and specifically asked me about the result. I didn't think much of it at the time and told him the truth. As a result, my brother concluded that you would hold significant power in the near future. He said that as long as we clung to you, we would definitely achieve great success in the future..."

"That son of a bitch! I'll curse his ancestors for eighteen generations!"

Timothy cursed in rage. Jadyn was truly an opportunist, relying on Austyn before, and now targeting himself. He wanted to climb the social ladder and reach the top in one step. Such wishful thinking! The most heartbreaking thing was that, in Jadyn's eyes, Austyn was nothing more than a tool.

Timothy lamented, "For his own future, that scoundrel is treating you like a plaything! If he had even a sliver of brotherly affection, no, if he had even a shred of human decency, he wouldn't do such despicable things!"

Austyn quickly stood up and covered Timothy's mouth, whispering, "Don't say it so loudly, someone might hear you."

Timothy spoke in a low voice, "Could it be that the person outside the window just now was also Jadyn?"

Austyn nodded, "I only dared to tell you this after seeing my brother leave."

"You can't go on like this, Austyn." Timothy couldn't stand it anymore, "Haven't you seen through Jadyn yet? He's a complete scoundrel! He doesn't love anyone, not even you. He only loves himself! Is such a person worth sacrificing yourself for?"

Austyn lowered his eyes in silence.

"I've decided." Timothy firmly grasped Austyn's hand and said softly, "Austyn, I'm going to take you away."

Austyn was startled and looked into Timothy's determined eyes.

"But you must promise me one thing," Timothy said, looking intently into Austyn's eyes.

"...What is it?" Austyn asked in confusion.

Timothy gave a sly smile and motioned for Austyn to come closer. As Austyn leaned in, they whispered into each other's ears.

The night sky, with its rolling clouds, was gradually giving way to dawn. At this moment, the brightest star in the sky twinkled, bringing a glimmer of hope to the lonely travelers of the long night.

As the night passed.

At the crack of dawn, Jadyn arrived at Qingchuan Residence, knocking on the door loudly. When no one responded, he shouted a few times, "Timothy."

Jadyn hesitated whether to enter when a lazy voice came from inside.

"Who is it, disturbing my sleep so early..."

It was Timothy's voice.

Jadyn quickly responded, "Timothy, it's me, Jadyn."

After he spoke, there was no response from inside, only the sound of rustling clothes.

After a while, the door creaked open. Timothy, with disheveled hair and a tired face, stood there with his shirt wide open, revealing his chiseled chest.

Timothy impatiently picked his ear, flicking the earwax away, "Why is it you?"

Jadyn was momentarily stunned but then smiled obsequiously, "I heard that Mr. Shaw got a sore throat from eating lychees, so I brought something to cool the heat for him."

Hearing this, Timothy noticed the servant behind Jadyn holding a large, round watermelon.

Timothy smiled, "That's nice, come in, come in."

He acted like the owner of Qingchuan Residence.

Inside, Jadyn instructed the servant to cut the watermelon for Timothy. Meanwhile, he walked to the bedroom door and peeked inside.

He saw a mess of clothes on the floor, and a slender, pale arm extending from the heavy curtains, hanging limply by the bed. Through the translucent curtains, the curves of a body were faintly visible...

Before he could take in the scene, a cough from behind made him turn around. He saw Timothy sitting casually in a chair with one leg propped up, looking very unrefined. Timothy rested his chin on one hand, his slightly upturned mouth showing a hint of mockery as he watched Jadyn.

"Mr. Brown, won't you try some?" Timothy pointed to the already cut watermelon.

Jadyn quickly sat down in the chair opposite Timothy.

Timothy, showing no concern for etiquette, started eating the watermelon himself and nodded, "This watermelon is good, very sweet."

Jadyn scrutinized Timothy for a while and then smiled, "Mr. Shaw, you look well today. Did you sleep well last night?"

Timothy quickly finished a slice of watermelon, wiped his mouth, and said, "You noticed that?"

He motioned for Jadyn to come closer. When Jadyn leaned in, Timothy whispered, "It was absolutely wonderful."

Even Jadyn, the instigator of this whole situation, blushed at Timothy's crude remark and laughed, "That's good, very good."

"Brother..."

As they whispered, a figure appeared silently beside them.

Jadyn saw Austyn, dressed in a thin robe, loosely tied at the waist, with his long black hair cascading down his back. Austyn seemed to have just woken up, his face still flushed. He walked slowly to Jadyn and bowed.

Jadyn was speechless, only staring at Austyn's exposed collarbone, where several love bites could be seen on his fair skin.

Timothy grabbed another slice of watermelon, pulling Austyn into his arms, "Austyn, this watermelon is sweet. Let me feed you."

Austyn, seemingly boneless, fell into Timothy's embrace with a slight tug. He gasped softly, clinging to Timothy's neck, "Don't tease me, this is in front of my brother..."

Timothy didn't care and pulled Austyn closer, letting him sit sideways on his lap, "So what if it's in front of your brother? Mr. Brown is not an outsider, right?"

Seeing Timothy's hint, Jadyn quickly nodded, "Of course, you two go ahead."

"That's more like it. Now, open your mouth, ah..." Timothy held a piece of watermelon to Austyn's lips. Austyn had no choice but to take a small bite.

"So sweet." Austyn chewed carefully, his eyes sparkling. He picked up a piece himself, "I want to feed you too, is that okay?"

"I'd love that, come on, ah—"

The two of them were so engrossed in feeding each other that it made Jadyn feel extremely awkward.

After indulging for a while, Timothy finally remembered Jadyn's presence, "Mr. Brown, time flies. Five days have passed in a blink. It's time for me to leave Mausoleum Rudolf and head to Poiema."

Jadyn looked regretful, "What a pity, I haven't had the chance to show you proper hospitality..."

Timothy quickly waved his hand, "You've been too kind already. Any more and I won't be able to handle it. But... there is one thing I can't leave behind."

"Oh? What is it?" Jadyn asked curiously.

Timothy lifted his head and exchanged a glance with Austyn, then smiled, "It's him."

Jadyn was stunned, not quite understanding.

"Mr. Brown, the great gift you've given me is exactly to my liking. I'm afraid if I leave now, I'll be lovesick and unable to eat or sleep, tormented day and night." As he spoke, Timothy pulled Austyn closer into his arms and smiled at Jadyn, "Since Mr. Brown was willing to give such a generous gift, surely you wouldn't be cruel enough to separate me from this beauty and let me suffer loneliness, right?"

"Well..."

Jadyn was at a loss for words. He seemed completely unprepared for Timothy's request, which left him flustered.

Seeing Jadyn's complex and conflicted expression, unable to make a decision, Timothy sat up straight and spoke earnestly, "Mr. Brown, let me put it this way. If I can have Austyn, I'll have your back in the future. If you need my help, I'll definitely oblige. I, Timothy, always keep my word."

Jadyn looked up at Timothy, then at Austyn.

Austyn turned his face away silently, lowering his eyes, his long eyelashes trembling slightly, and clenched his fists on his knees.

He knew that his fate depended on this moment.

Jadyn hesitated for a long time before finally speaking with difficulty, "Let me think about it, Timothy."

Timothy smiled slightly and said heartily, "Alright! I'll give you one more day. Mr. Brown, this concerns your future, so you must think it over carefully."

Timothy had posed a difficult question for Jadyn. Whether to let go of Austyn or not, Jadyn couldn't decide right away. While Jadyn was facing this life-and-death decision, his confidant Urijah was also facing a different kind of life-and-death dilemma.

In the courtyard of Dawsyn's mansion, Urijah, beaten black and blue, lay weakly in a corner, desperately begging Adam for mercy. "Brother, we have no past grievances or recent hatred, why are you beating me for no reason!"

"Shut up!" Adam stepped forward, grabbed him by the collar, and demanded fiercely, "What's your relationship with Timothy?"

To understand why Adam and Urijah were entangled, it all started with Urijah's marital status in Mausoleum Rudolf. Urijah was married to Dawsyn's daughter, Julia Clarke. So, technically, Urijah was Dawsyn's son-in-law.

Since Urijah was demoted to a commoner and returned to Mausoleum Rudolf, the Rogers family had been arranging a marriage for him. Due to Urijah's bad reputation, no normal family would want to marry their daughter to him. So, when the Rogers family first approached Dawsyn, he refused. But after persistent pleading, he finally agreed to let the young couple meet.

Unexpectedly, Julia and Urijah hit it off immediately. Despite Dawsyn's objections, Julia insisted on marrying Urijah.

Seeing his daughter's determination, Dawsyn reluctantly agreed to the marriage and gave his daughter away with mixed feelings.

In the first month of their marriage, Urijah and Julia's relationship was harmonious, and their days were sweet. But as the saying goes, old habits die hard. Over time, Urijah's restless heart began to stir again. He frequently visited brothels and stayed out all night, leaving Julia alone.

Julia, being impulsive and strong-willed, returned to her parents' home in anger, locked herself in her room, and refused to see anyone.

Urijah, having no other choice, went to the Clarke family to persuade his wife to return. Coincidentally, he ran into Adam, who was a guest at the Clarke residence.

As the saying goes, enemies often cross paths. Adam immediately recognized Urijah as the man tied up by Timothy in the attic. Suspecting an improper relationship between Urijah and Timothy, Adam couldn't contain his anger and decided to teach Urijah a lesson on behalf of Miss Pu.

Urijah, unable to withstand the beating, quickly begged for mercy and confessed everything about his encounter with Timothy, detailing how it all happened.

Only then did Adam realize he had wronged Timothy.

To verify Urijah's testimony, Adam also questioned the two guards who had been with Timothy that day. Their accounts matched Urijah's, confirming he hadn't lied.

Knowing there was nothing suspicious between Timothy and Urijah, Adam finally breathed a sigh of relief. In fact, if he had calmly talked to Timothy that day and given him a chance to explain, perhaps there wouldn't have been such a misunderstanding.

While it was easy to say, the problem was that Adam found it increasingly difficult to stay calm in front of Timothy.

With these conflicting feelings, Adam finally gathered the courage to return to Shaw Mansion two days after running away from home.

Chapter Forty: Confession

As the saying goes, a day apart feels like three years. Adam, who had left in anger, started missing Timothy after just two days apart. Now that Adam had returned to the Western Garden, he saw the light still on in the west wing, indicating that Timothy had not yet gone to bed, which made him both happy and anxious.

He was happy because they were reuniting after a brief separation, but anxious because he didn't know how to face Timothy. Should he apologize and say sorry for the misunderstanding? Or should he act as if nothing had happened?

Adam was still hesitating outside when a voice came from within.

"Who's out there?"

It was Timothy's voice!

Adam was startled and instinctively turned to leave, but the door opened with a bang.

"Adam!?"

Even with his back turned, Adam could hear the surprise and joy in Timothy's voice. Timothy didn't give Adam a chance to run away, grabbing his hand.

With no escape, Adam turned around.

"You're not mad at me anymore?" Timothy's voice was incredibly gentle, with a hint of tentative hope.

"I..." Adam stammered, "I'm not mad at you."

"Not mad?" Timothy laughed, "Then explain to me what 'old sly fox' means?"

Adam's face turned beet red. He knew Timothy would tease him about this. In a fit of embarrassment, he yanked his hand away from Timothy and said, "You heard wrong! I'm tired! I'm going to bed!"

Ignoring Timothy's attempts to stop him, Adam bolted into the bedroom.

The moment he lifted the quilt on the bed, Adam froze.

Timothy also rushed in, but it was too late.

Lying under the covers was a man dressed in thin clothing. He seemed to have been awakened by the commotion, blinking sleepily at Adam, looking bewildered. It was none other than Austyn.

The three of them stared at each other, the atmosphere growing increasingly awkward.

Austyn was the first to recover. He sat up lazily, covering his mouth as he yawned, and greeted Adam without a hint of tension.

"Mr. Garcia, you're back?"

"You, you... you two!" Adam finally snapped out of it. He took a few steps back, looking from Austyn to Timothy, "You actually got together!?"

Timothy sighed, "Adam, this is a misunderstanding..."

"What kind of misunderstanding!? He's in your bed!!"

"But didn't we always sleep together before?"

Timothy's words left Adam speechless.

Austyn stepped in to help, "Mr. Garcia, I'm playing a role in a play with you."

"A play?" Adam tilted his head in confusion, "What play? For whom?"

"Who else but Jadyn could we be putting on a show for here at Shaw Mansion?" Timothy put his arm around Adam's shoulders, "As for the name of this play, let's call it 'Plotting.'"

Adam frowned, "What are you two talking about? I don't understand any of this."

Timothy stopped playing games with Adam and sat him down next to Austyn, explaining the plan he and Austyn had devised the previous night.

"Wait, let me get this straight." After listening to Timothy, Adam's head was spinning. He rubbed his temples, "So, Jadyn sent Master Powell to seduce you, and you're using Jadyn's future as leverage to make him release Master Powell?"

"Exactly." Timothy nodded, "If we're going to act, we need to make it convincing. If Austyn and I didn't share a bed, how could we fool Jadyn, that old fox?"

"I understand the logic... but..." Adam glanced at Austyn, hesitant to speak.

Austyn, being perceptive, quickly understood Adam's thoughts and reassured him, "Mr. Garcia, don't worry. This act is only temporary. Austyn is just borrowing your beloved for a while. When the play is over, I'll return him to you."

"Beloved..." Adam's face turned crimson, and he jumped up, "Master Powell! What nonsense are you spouting!? I... I don't have a beloved!"

Austyn remained confident, "Austyn's judgment of people is always accurate, never wrong."

"Austyn," Timothy, extremely embarrassed, quickly pulled Austyn aside and whispered, "Some things are best left unspoken."

"Unspoken?" Austyn smiled faintly, "Unspoken only to you, perhaps?"

Now Timothy was the one left speechless.

Adam, unable to hear their whispering, sat there blushing and feeling increasingly uncomfortable. He was about to leave when Timothy grabbed his arm.

"Adam, wait!"

Timothy had long sensed Adam's feelings for him, but because Adam never spoke up, he pretended not to notice. Now, with Austyn unexpectedly bringing it out into the open, the secret they had both carefully hidden in their hearts was laid bare, forcing them to confront their true feelings.

Timothy realized Austyn was right. He was always proactive in life, but when it came to Adam, he had been passive and complacent.

Now, hearing Austyn's words, Timothy suddenly understood something important. He had been ignoring his own true feelings.

When you like something, you must go after it, even if it means taking a risk. That's how he had always been, hadn't he?

So this time, Timothy decided to face his feelings directly and express what was truly in his heart.

"There's something I've been holding in for a long, long time. I've wanted to tell you for a while now." Timothy looked Adam in the eye, speaking seriously.

Adam's heart raced. The usual roguishness was gone from Timothy's face, replaced by an unprecedented seriousness. Adam panicked. Could Timothy have already seen through his feelings? Was he going to cut ties with him?

Adam grew more anxious, his mind racing with a hundred different ways Timothy might reject him.

"No, don't say it!" Adam covered his ears, shaking his head, "I don't want to hear it!"

Timothy pulled his hands away from his ears, pressing Adam onto the bed, and shouted—

"I want you!"

Adam was stunned, and even Austyn beside him froze.

Timothy remained unfazed. He took a deep breath and looked into Adam's eyes, "I want to hold you, kiss you, and I can't stop thinking about you every day."

Adam stared blankly at Timothy, as if his soul had been pulled out, unable to react.

"Where's your soul?" Austyn waved his hand in front of Adam's face and then looked up at Timothy, "I've never seen anyone get so flustered by a love confession before."

Timothy was puzzled, "Did I not make myself clear?"

"You made it too clear." Austyn chuckled, "I really can't handle you two. Let me help you out."

With that, Austyn moved behind Adam, lifting him up in a hug.

"Ah!" Adam finally snapped back to reality, flailing in panic, "Master Powell, what are you doing... mmph!?"

Adam's protest was cut short as Timothy leaned in and kissed him. Sandwiched between Timothy and Austyn, Adam could only let out a muffled groan.

As Timothy kissed him, he slipped his hand under Adam's shirt, gently teasing his chest.

"I like you, Adam."

The breathy confession, mixed with soft kisses, carried an undeniable desire, piercing through Adam's heart. His body trembled, and his resistance melted away under Timothy's touch.

When Timothy finally released his lips, Adam was left breathless, collapsing into Austyn's arms, gasping for air like a fish out of water.

"Is this... a dream?" Adam asked dazedly.

"It's not a dream." Timothy, breathing heavily, quickly undid his belt, "I'll make you see that soon."

A cool breeze stirred the curtains, casting gentle movements in the pitch-black silence of the night. No one would imagine the scandalous scene unfolding in the west wing of Shaw Mansion.

Timothy stood at the edge of the bed, his shirt wide open, baring his lower half. Before him, with legs spread wide and allowing Timothy's rod to thrust freely into his dripping hole, was the naked Adam.

"How about this, Adam?" Timothy asked, thrusting shallowly at first, then pushing deeper, grinding patiently against the sensitive inner walls, and then slowly pulling out. "Do you like it when I do this to you?"

"I love it... harder, deeper!"

Adam's body twisted restlessly, his greedy hole tightening around Timothy, wetly expelling juices. It had been a long time since Timothy had seen Adam show such lasciviousness in front of him. Unable to restrain himself any longer, he thrust his hips forward, burying himself completely inside Adam, hitting the sweet spot that made Adam cry out in ecstasy. Grasping Adam's waist, Timothy began to pound him forcefully, without hesitation.

Meanwhile, Austyn, kneeling behind Adam, gently cradled Adam's head in his lap. Austyn was still clad in a single robe, though it hung more loosely now, revealing the enticing curves of his collarbone under a cascade of hair.

As Timothy's hips moved with relentless rhythm, thrusting in and out of Adam's tight entrance, his eyes locked onto Austyn. It was a gaze filled with raw, animalistic desire, making Austyn feel like prey under a predator's watchful eye. Embarrassed and nervous, he turned his head away.

Though they were only acting, Timothy had promised Austyn that, despite sharing the bed at night, he would never touch him without permission.

Even though Austyn's own desire had become painfully erect.

"Do you like me, Adam?"

"I love you... I love you..."

Adam's mouth had been open since the beginning, uttering nothing but moans and the instinctual declaration of "love," stripped of any shame or modesty. His body arched in a graceful curve, hanging in mid-air, his legs wrapped around Timothy's waist, eagerly anticipating Timothy's deeper, faster thrusts.

Austyn had never witnessed such an intimate act between two men at such close quarters. The sight was incredibly overwhelming. As a bystander, he felt both a sense of taboo and shame, but he couldn't tear his eyes away from the sight of Timothy's thick rod plunging into the tight, welcoming flesh, producing a frothy mix at the point of their union.

Suddenly, Austyn felt a sharp pain in his arm. It was Adam's hand, which had found no place to rest and had gripped Austyn's arm, the nails digging deeply into his flesh.

"So deep..."

Adam shook his head wildly, his lower abdomen convulsing with sudden spasms.

Seeing this, Timothy took a deep breath, pressed down on Adam's hips, and thrust hard into his hole.

"Ah! You hit it!!"

With Timothy hitting his sweet spot, Adam's eyes rolled back in pleasure, and his erection began to spurt wildly, shooting streams of white.

Austyn felt parched, instinctively licking his lips as he watched. His hand slid down, reaching into his pants to stroke his own swollen desire.

Unbeknownst to Austyn, even in the dark, Timothy could see his every move. Austyn also didn't realize that his unconscious moans only stoked Timothy's lust further.

"Ugh..."

Austyn's rod, always sensitive, quickly neared climax, just as Timothy, after thrusting hundreds of times into Adam, was ready to release. As Austyn came, Timothy's member twitched, and he shot his load deep into Adam's slick, clenching hole.

Suddenly, Timothy reached out and grabbed Austyn by the neck.

Austyn instinctively leaned in, their lips meeting in a passionate kiss as his hand was coated with his own sticky seed.

Chapter Forty-One: Severing Ties

Since you knew I liked you, why didn't you say anything sooner!? Afterward, when Adam asked this question with a mix of resentment and embarrassment, Timothy found himself at a loss for words.

Talking about respecting Adam's choices sounded like a pretty excuse. The truth was, Timothy found it amusing, like observing a cute little animal. Watching Adam be happy or worried for him, watching Adam throw little fits and get angry at him, all of it delighted him and satisfied Timothy's curiosity.

Adam genuinely cared for him and worried about him, but Timothy had treated him as an amusing pet. Thinking about it this way, Timothy felt a bit ashamed.

Gratitude towards Austyn welled up within him. If it weren't for Austyn, Timothy might still be smugly enjoying his superior position as an observer.

Of course, credit must also go to Urijah. Though Timothy didn't want to admit it, Urijah, despite being a lustful creature, had his uses. If you pressed him, you could always extract some valuable information from his loose lips.

Timothy was indeed shocked when he learned Urijah had a wife. Upon further inquiry, he discovered Urijah's connection to Dawsyn. But what surprised him even more was that this man named Dawsyn had a tear-jerking story of bitterness with Jadyn. In Mausoleum Rudolf, most people were deceived by Jadyn's appearance. Only a handful knew Jadyn's true nature, and Dawsyn was one of them.

If Timothy guessed correctly, the person who really saved Dawsyn's youngest son was Austyn. He wondered how Dawsyn would react if he knew the truth.

When Timothy shared this thought with Adam, Adam was silent for a long time before saying, "I think we should tell him. Mr. Clarke would want to know the truth."

Dawsyn recognized Timothy almost instantly.

When Timothy and Adam appeared before Dawsyn, his cloudy eyes suddenly cleared, sparkling with excitement.

"I know you, the one from Temple Kalpana... you're Timothy!!"

Although Timothy had heard about Dawsyn before arriving, being regarded with such reverence by a stranger still left him feeling flattered.

After servants brought hot tea and the three exchanged pleasantries, Timothy got straight to the point.

"Mr. Clarke. Have you ever heard of a person named Austyn?"

"Austyn...?" As expected, Dawsyn looked utterly confused.

Timothy and Adam exchanged glances. It seemed Jadyn had hidden Austyn well. Although Austyn had come to Mausoleum Rudolf with Jadyn and had done so much behind the scenes for both Jadyn and the people, no one knew of his existence.

So Timothy didn't hold back and recounted the story of Jadyn and Austyn's relationship, how they entered service, and how Jadyn used Austyn to climb the ranks, deceiving the entire populace of Mausoleum Rudolf.

After listening silently, Dawsyn's face turned pale, and his hand holding the teacup trembled slightly. "So, the one who truly healed my son was not Jadyn..."

"That's right." Timothy looked Dawsyn in the eye and said, "It was Austyn."

Dawsyn let out a long sigh, a look of guilt crossing his face. "No wonder I always felt something was off about Mr. Brown. Your explanation makes everything clear. Mr. Shaw, if it weren't for your honesty, I would still be in the dark, not even knowing my son's true savior. I'm deeply ashamed."

Not wanting to see Dawsyn blame himself, Adam quickly consoled him, "Mr. Clarke, you shouldn't be too hard on yourself. You're far better than those who can't distinguish right from wrong."

"Adam is right," Timothy nodded. "In this Mausoleum Rudolf, there aren't many like Mr. Clarke who can calmly see through Jadyn's facade."

"Actually, it's not that simple," Dawsyn shook his head, glanced around, and lowered his voice. "You may not know, but ever since the government started conscripting musicians from Kamal, more and more people have become discontented with Jadyn, especially the Four Great Families of Mausoleum Rudolf."

Timothy's eyes lit up. "So the conscription orders came from Jadyn?"

Dawsyn nodded. "Officially, it's to resist the nomads, but everyone knows it's just an excuse. Jadyn merely wants to amass power. The Four Great Families have long had grudges against him, and now that he's undermining their foundations, they can't stand him."

"I thought the whole Mausoleum Rudolf supported Jadyn. Turns out he's not so popular," Adam said, feeling quite vindicated. "Right, Alan?"

But Timothy, deep in thought, remained silent for a long time.

"Alan? What's on your mind?" Adam nudged his shoulder.

Timothy snapped out of his reverie and looked at Dawsyn. "Mr. Clarke, to be honest, I am about to undertake something significant, something that concerns the lives and futures of the people of Mausoleum Rudolf. I need your help. Would you be willing to assist me?"

Seeing Timothy's serious expression, Dawsyn knew it was a matter of great importance. He sat up straight, resolutely saying, "Mr. Shaw, just tell me what you need. As long as it's within my power, I won't refuse."

While Timothy and Adam discussed plans with Dawsyn outside the city, Austyn lounged by the pool at Qingchuan Residence, holding a fishing rod, letting the dappled afternoon sunlight fall on his face.

Austyn had dozed off, dreaming of a time over a decade ago when he was a child, traveling with his master and brother through mountains and rivers. He remembered chasing his brother in the open fields and sneaking up on his sleeping master to pluck a white hair from his beard.

In the dream, he felt genuine happiness and smiled brightly at his brother.

Though it felt real, it was just a dream.

The rustling of footsteps on fallen leaves interrupted Austyn's light slumber. His lashes fluttered as he slowly opened his eyes.

"Where's Timothy? Why are you alone?" The voice he least wanted to hear sounded from above.

Austyn's heart sank, as if he had fallen from the heavens to the earth.

"Let me guess, Adam is back, and Timothy, favoring his old love over the new, has abandoned you?" Jadyn's tone was full of mockery.

Austyn sat up expressionlessly and replied in a detached voice, "What do you want, brother?"

"Nothing much," Jadyn sat beside Austyn, tilting his head to look at him. "Just checking what you're up to."

Austyn kept his gaze fixed on the bobber floating on the water, not intending to engage with Jadyn.

"Are you still angry with me?"

"No."

"Really?"

"..."

"Then why do you look like you don't want to talk to me?"

".........."

"I know you resent me, saying you'll leave with Timothy just to spite me, right?"

Austyn finally couldn't hold back anymore and stood up abruptly. "I'm leaving with Timothy because I like him. It has nothing to do with you."

Jadyn also stood up, his sharp eyes fixed on Austyn's profile. "Then why don't you dare look me in the eyes and say that?"

Hearing this, Austyn slowly turned his head. His dark eyes seemed like deep whirlpools, filled with complex emotions.

"You made me seduce him, and now you're forbidding me from being with him. To you, Austyn is just a plaything, summoned and dismissed at your whim. You don't care what I think or what I want, so why pretend to care now?"

Austyn's words, held back for so long, poured out in a torrent, brutally honest and leaving no face for Jadyn. Jadyn's expression faltered, his face turning a shade of humiliation.

But Austyn wasn't done. He paused, then continued, "But Timothy is different. I like Timothy, and he likes me too. More than that, he understands me, respects me, and never forces me to do anything I don't want to do. He is everything good, and most importantly..."

Austyn took a deep breath and uttered four resolute words: "He has integrity."

Jadyn's face flickered with emotion, turning red and then white, leaving him speechless.

Seeing Jadyn silenced, Austyn felt a surge of satisfaction. He turned to leave, but an enraged Jadyn grabbed his hand.

"Stop right there!" Jadyn yanked Austyn back and roughly pushed him against the trunk of the willow tree. "Just because you were fucked once, you think you can turn against me? You little slut, stop pretending to be so pure!"

Austyn's head hit the tree trunk hard, causing him to gasp in pain.

But Jadyn paid no heed to Austyn's discomfort, continuing his verbal assault. "What love? You think I don't know? You're just sticking with Timothy to curry favor with him, hoping for future success!"

"That's you, isn't it? Brother!" Austyn's face turned pale as if he had suffered a great insult, his lips trembling. "What gives you the right to assume there's no genuine feeling between Timothy and me? Do you think the world is just about using each other and there's no room for true emotions?"

"Because you are mine!" Jadyn punched the tree trunk, shouting angrily.

Austyn bit his lip, staring coldly at Jadyn.

Jadyn grabbed Austyn's shoulders, speaking in a falsely gentle tone. "Austyn, you were so adorable as a child, like a little tail following me everywhere, always wanting to be held. Then you grew up and started talking back to me. But it's okay, I, as your brother, was tolerant of your willfulness. Later, you became more disobedient and began to compete with me. Yes, you are smart and lovable, and everyone dotes on you. Even our master passed the mantle to you. Did I ever complain?"

The insidious words penetrated Austyn's ears, each venomous statement seeping into his blood and bones, constricting his heart until he could barely breathe.

"Stop it..."

Austyn covered his ears, struggling to escape, trying to block out the invading voice.

But Jadyn wouldn't let him go so easily. He pressed Austyn firmly against the tree, bringing his lips close to Austyn's ear. "Austyn, I've always treated you well, but what about you? You've changed. The once content and peaceful you now chases fame and fortune."

Jadyn sighed deeply, feigning regret. "I came today to test you. If you had said, 'I want to stay by your side,' I would have let you go. After all, parting is only temporary. As long as you still think of me as your brother, we would eventually be together again. But you chose the wrong answer."

A dry laugh escaped Austyn's throat, his heart plunging into icy depths.

Fifteen years of companionship felt like a cruel joke. All the bonds of brotherhood and friendship he had cherished were meaningless. The treasure he held so dear was worthless in the eyes of the one he respected most, to be trampled and discarded at will.

It was time to end this.

"Let go."

"What?"

"I said, let go!"

Austyn summoned a sudden burst of strength and pushed Jadyn back a few steps.

"Austyn, you...!"

"From today onwards, we are done!" Austyn's voice was hoarse as he forced the words out. "You are no longer my brother, and you will never control me again!"

When Austyn looked up again, the last trace of warmth in his eyes had vanished, leaving only an abyss of coldness.

Jadyn was stunned, a sense of unprecedented crisis welling up inside him. As he watched Austyn turn decisively away, a terrible premonition arose within him. If he didn't reach out now, Austyn would disappear from his life forever.

This was not a temporary parting. He knew, as Austyn had declared, from this moment on, Austyn no longer belonged to him.

With a swift movement, a shadow dropped behind Austyn, raising a hand knife to strike at the back of his neck.

Austyn collapsed silently, falling limply into the arms of the black-clad guard.

"Mr. Brown!" The guard turned, bowing to Jadyn.

Jadyn walked over slowly, gazing at the unconscious Austyn. He gently stroked Austyn's cheek and murmured, "Since you refused the kind offer, don't blame your brother for serving you the harsh one."

Chapter Forty-Two: The Incident at Mausoleum Rudolf

"Austyn refuses to come with me? Did he really say that?" Timothy looked skeptical.

"I tried to persuade him, but he can't bear to leave the people of Mausoleum Rudolf. He says he has grown attached to them," Jadyn replied, still wearing a friendly smile, apologizing profusely to Timothy. "So this time, Austyn won't be able to go with you."

"How could that be..." Adam was about to retort when Timothy quickly covered his mouth.

Timothy smiled nonchalantly. "I see. If that's what Austyn wants, I won't force him. But before I leave, I'd like to see Austyn one last time to thank him for his care over these days."

"Well..." Jadyn looked troubled. "I'm afraid that's a bit inconvenient. As you know, Austyn hasn't been feeling well recently and has already gone to rest. It's best not to disturb him."

Timothy pondered for a moment, then sighed. "Alright. I'll take my leave then."

"I won't keep you," Jadyn said, bowing respectfully.

Timothy, holding Adam, quickly left Shaw Mansion, ignoring Adam's muffled protests.

Once they were some distance away, Timothy finally let go of Adam. Adam took a deep breath, his face flushed with anger.

"Alan! Why did you just leave? Jadyn is obviously hiding something!"

"I know." Timothy's expression was serious, his brow furrowed deeply. "Austyn is not someone who goes back on his word. We agreed he'd help me finish this act; there's no way he'd give up so easily."

"Then why aren't you rescuing him? That Jadyn wouldn't even let us see Master Powell. If we delay any longer, Master Powell might already be..."

"Stop talking nonsense," Timothy interrupted, "Words have power. Don't jinx it."

Adam glared at Timothy. "Aren't you worried about Master Powell? I thought you liked him."

"Of course I'm worried, but we can't just rush in blindly. We need a well-thought-out plan."

"You're not denying it, so you really do like him..." Adam muttered.

Timothy ignored him, thinking aloud, "If Jadyn won't let Austyn go with me, it means he needs him. So Austyn should be safe for now. The key is to find out where he's being held. If someone could sneak into Shaw Mansion and get us some information, that would be ideal..."

Adam, following Timothy's train of thought, suddenly brightened. "I know someone who might help, though I'm not sure if he's reliable."

"Who?" Timothy asked.

"Urijah. Didn't you say he's Jadyn's drinking buddy?"

After being beaten by Adam and kneeling outside the Clarke residence for a night, Urijah finally softened Julia's heart and brought her back to the Rogers family. Fearful of another beating from Adam, Urijah had been keeping a low profile, staying away from brothels and trying to keep busy with chores, as Julia frequently assigned him tasks to keep him occupied. When Timothy and Adam found him, he was in the garden, wrestling with a flock of hens.

"Urijah?" Timothy could hardly believe his eyes.

Seeing Timothy, Urijah blushed, tossed aside the struggling hen, and ran over with feathers sticking to his hair.

"Timothy—"

The drawn-out whine was sugary enough to give anyone cavities, but before he could finish, Adam stepped in, looking like a fierce guardian.

Urijah quickly straightened up, his flirty demeanor vanishing. "What can I do for you?"

It was evening, and Timothy and Adam had come at just the right time to enjoy a hearty chicken soup meal at the Rogers family table. Julia, grateful for Adam's intervention, treated Timothy as a friend and served them generously.

As Timothy devoured a juicy drumstick, he advised Urijah to cherish his kind wife. Under Adam's intimidating glare, Urijah meekly agreed.

After dinner, Timothy pulled Urijah aside and asked if he knew Austyn. Urijah nodded, saying he'd met him once at Shaw Mansion. Timothy was thrilled and asked Urijah to go to Shaw Mansion and discreetly find out Austyn's whereabouts and condition. Timothy had expected some resistance from Urijah, given their past, but Urijah agreed surprisingly readily. In truth, Urijah had been itching to get out of the house, and Timothy's request provided the perfect excuse.

Knowing Urijah's nature, Timothy didn't have high expectations, but Urijah kept his promise. One day, he arrived at Shaw Mansion with a jar of fine wine.

As Jadyn's drinking buddy, Urijah often joined him for feasts. But today, Jadyn seemed different. From the moment Urijah sat down, Jadyn was silent, drinking heavily and frowning, clearly troubled.

Urijah took note, chatting casually while steering the conversation towards Austyn.

"Mr. Brown, ever since I met Master Powell at Shaw Mansion, I haven't been able to forget him."

"Oh?" Jadyn scoffed, his breath reeking of alcohol. "I didn't think Urijah would lust after Austyn too."

"You know me, Mr. Brown. Having such a beauty by my side every day would make me the envy of everyone. How could there be such an otherworldly person in this world?"

Jadyn sneered. "Otherworldly? Divine? You're overthinking it." He downed his drink and slammed the cup on the table, muttering, "He's just a whore, fickle and faithless."

"That's perfect!" Urijah clapped, quickly covering his tracks under Jadyn's glare. "No, no, I mean, I love hearing such gossip. Mr. Brown, indulge my curiosity."

Jadyn glanced at Urijah. "You're a womanizer, always chasing skirts. You'd be a perfect match for my brother."

Urijah laughed. "Mr. Brown flatters me. I'm just a common man, unworthy of your divine brother. But if I had the chance to get close to Master Powell, I'd die a thousand times over, happily."

Jadyn squinted at Urijah, silent for a long time. "What if I said you had that chance?"

Urijah followed Jadyn through winding corridors and courtyards, arriving at an inconspicuous room in a remote corner of Shaw Mansion. This secluded area, once the servants' quarters, was now deserted, save for a solitary lamp flickering weakly inside.

Jadyn unlocked the heavy iron lock and pushed open the door. Austyn stood by the wall, absorbed in the symbols and writings covering it.

Since being confined here, Austyn had passed the time by picking up sticks from the pile of wood in the corner, writing and calculating on the bare walls.

Seeing Jadyn enter, Austyn's heart briefly lit up with hope, only to extinguish when he saw who followed him.

Jadyn belched. "Brother, do you remember him?"

Austyn turned away from Jadyn's reeking breath, disgusted.

"Master Powell!" Urijah stepped forward, smiling. "It's Urijah. Do you remember me?"

Austyn took a step back, eyeing Urijah warily. "I remember. So what?"

Jadyn snorted. "Urijah said he'd die happy just to get close to you."

Austyn was momentarily stunned, then his face paled as he looked at Jadyn in disbelief. "What did you say..."

"Didn't you say you like Timothy and Timothy likes you too?" Jadyn's face broke into a teasing smile. "Don't be foolish. When Timothy knew you wouldn't leave with him, he didn't even ask a question, just turned around and left. He doesn't care about you at all."

Faced with Jadyn's provocation, Austyn chose silence. He turned his face away, lips tightly pressed together. However, his slightly trembling body betrayed the helplessness in his heart.

"How ridiculous. You didn't really fall for him, did you?" Jadyn, like a victor, looked down at Austyn with eyes full of pity. "What is love worth? A few measly bucks? Look at yourself in the mirror. You look like an abandoned wife!"

Austyn's face had long since turned pale, and even Urijah, watching from the side, couldn't help but feel a pang of sympathy.

"It's just a man. There are plenty of men in this world besides Timothy." With that, Jadyn grabbed Urijah's shoulder. "Look at Urijah, isn't he also handsome and talented? How is he any worse than Timothy? If you're lonely, Urijah can satisfy you too. Right, Urijah?"

Though the atmosphere made Urijah a bit uncomfortable, he nodded vigorously. "Of course!"

"That's the spirit!" Jadyn patted his shoulder and whispered in his ear, "I know your skills. Comfort him well for me and make him forget Timothy soon."

Before Urijah could respond, Jadyn laughed loudly and turned to leave.

The door closed with a bang and was locked from the outside. Urijah was startled, rushing to the door and pounding on it. "Mr. Brown!? Why did you lock me in here too?"

Jadyn's voice came from outside. "Don't worry, have your fun. I'll come back to unlock it in an hour."

"You can't be serious, Mr. Brown! Mr. Brown!?"

Urijah banged on the door furiously, but there was no response outside. He couldn't tell if Jadyn was serious or just joking, leaving him utterly confused.

As soon as Urijah turned around, everything went black, and with a thud, he was hit on the forehead.

"Ouch!" Urijah clutched his forehead, seeing stars, and looked up to see Austyn holding a wooden stick, swinging it towards his face again.

Reflexively, Urijah ducked his head, dodging the second strike, and lunged forward, tightly hugging Austyn's waist.

"Master Powell! Let's talk this out, don't resort to violence!"

"Let go of me!" Austyn, a frail Taoist priest with no martial arts skills, wielded the thick wooden stick clumsily, hitting Urijah's back aimlessly.

Fortunately, Austyn's strength was weak, and although his actions seemed fierce, the blows weren't too heavy. If it were Timothy or Adam, that first strike would have knocked Urijah out cold.

Austyn's lack of strength gave Urijah a chance to retaliate. He pushed forward, pinning Austyn to the ground, causing the stick to fall from his hand.

Using the skills and momentum he had when fighting chickens during the day, Urijah grabbed Austyn's flailing hands, pinning them firmly to the ground.

"Don't come any closer!" Austyn's voice trembled with genuine fear, his teary eyes fixed on Urijah.

Urijah felt a rush of heat in his heart. If not for Timothy's stern warnings echoing in his mind, he might have lost control of himself.

"Timothy sent me!" Urijah shouted.

"What...?" Austyn was stunned, stopping his struggle.

"I'm sorry, Urijah. I acted impulsively earlier."

Once the misunderstanding was cleared, Austyn, filled with guilt, bowed deeply to Urijah.

Sitting side by side against the wall, Urijah waved his hand while touching his swollen forehead. "Forget it. It's not your fault. If anyone's to blame, it's Timothy. When I get out, I must complain to him. This is a ridiculous errand! If I weren't so lucky, I would have been dead by now. And now, I'm locked up in here, the one who came to gather information. Are we really going to wait here for an hour?"

"Judging by Jadyn's drunken state, he might forget all about it. Whether we'll get out in an hour is uncertain." Austyn said softly.

Urijah wondered, "Aren't you two brothers? How did things end up like this?"

Austyn's dry lips curled slightly. "It's a long story."

Curious, Urijah looked at Austyn's profile. "Master Powell, did you really sleep with Timothy?"

Austyn blushed, turning away. "That's none of your business."

"I can't be curious even if it's none of my business?" Urijah moved closer, shaking Austyn's arm. "Master Powell, we have an hour to kill. Talk to me, or else..."

Urijah's tone shifted, his eyes gleaming. "I might not be able to control myself."

Austyn stiffened, his face turning pale.

Seeing Austyn's reaction, Urijah burst into laughter. "Look at you! Relax, I wouldn't dare do anything to you. If Timothy found out, he'd tear me apart, like last time..."

"Last time?" Austyn asked, puzzled.

Laughing heartily, Urijah said, "I brought it upon myself, lusting after Timothy's lover. Tried to sneak a taste, but ended up being tied up and whipped all night by Timothy."

Originally, Urijah wanted to get some gossip about Timothy from Austyn. Instead, he ended up spilling his own embarrassing history.

Time passed unknowingly.

Austyn's prediction came true. An hour later, Jadyn hadn't returned. Urijah started to worry, thinking that Jadyn might indeed have gotten drunk and forgotten about them.

"Should we try to escape?" Urijah stood up, searching the room. "We can't stay here all night."

"Don't waste your effort. I've searched the room already. There's nothing useful for escape."

"This place is so secure, not even a window." Urijah looked around, then up, spotting a small skylight. "The only exit is up there."

"Can you reach that high?" Austyn asked.

Urijah shrugged, and they fell silent again.

Suddenly, they heard faint commotion outside.

"What's happening? Is there something going on outside?" Urijah frowned.

Austyn also heard it, moving to the door and pressing his ear against it to listen closely. "Sounds like shouting."

"Could there be a fire?" Urijah's heart tightened. "We might be stuck here while something happens outside!"

Austyn remained calm. "Stay calm. It doesn't sound like a fire. There are sounds of weapons clashing..."

Urijah's face turned pale. "That doesn't sound good either, Master Powell!"

"Shh!" Austyn raised a finger, signaling Urijah to be quiet. He listened for a while longer, his expression darkening. "Someone's coming this way!"

"What!?" Urijah panicked. "Are they coming to kill me? Did Jadyn find out I was sent by Timothy!?"

Rapid footsteps approached, followed by the sound of a key turning in the lock. The door was flung open.

It was Jadyn. He burst in, not even glancing at Urijah, and grabbed Austyn's hand. "Come with me!"

Austyn was stunned, then began to struggle.

"Let go! Where are you taking me!?"

Seeing this, Urijah mustered his courage and rushed forward to block Jadyn.

"Mr. Brown, what's going on?"

Jadyn's face was grim. "There's trouble outside. The rebels are almost here!"

"Rebels?" Urijah and Austyn were both shocked.

"Urijah, you shouldn't stay here either. Run, hide, do whatever you want, I can't help you anymore. As for Austyn..." Jadyn stared at Austyn. "You must come with me today!"

With that, Jadyn started to drag Austyn out. Desperate, Urijah used his last resort, clinging to Jadyn's waist.

"Mr. Brown! What kind of friendship do we have? How can you be so cold and heartless? Drinking and laughing with me one moment, and kicking me to the curb the next, leaving me to fend for myself. I don't agree!"

Jadyn was fed up with Urijah's clinging. Unlike Austyn, he had no sympathy for Urijah and kicked him away.

With a thud, Urijah's head hit the threshold, and he lost consciousness.

Chapter Forty-Three: Utter Defeat

The flames illuminated the night sky of Mausoleum Rudolf like daylight. Amidst the continuous sounds of shouting and killing, Jadyn, surrounded by dozens of guards, dragged a bewildered Austyn onto the carriage parked at the back door of Shaw Mansion.

"Quick! Head out through the south gate!" Jadyn shouted to the guard driving the carriage.

"Mr. Brown, the road to the south gate is blocked by the rebels. We can't get through," the guard replied.

Jadyn frowned slightly. "Then the north gate."

"The battle is fierce in the north. It's extremely dangerous," the guard vetoed Jadyn's suggestion again. "Not just the north, all routes to the four gates have been blocked by the Four Great Families."

"This won't do, that won't do either!" Jadyn finally couldn't suppress his anger and exploded. "Are you saying we should just wait here to die?"

"N-no, that's not what I mean!"

"Your duty is to protect me at all costs! Even if there's danger, we have to break through. Otherwise, what use are you to me?" Jadyn waved his hand and said, "Stop wasting time, head to the north gate."

"Yes!"

The horse neighed loudly and pulled the carriage, galloping down the cobblestone road.

Inside the swaying carriage, Austyn stared silently at the man in front of him. Jadyn's face was tense, deep lines etched into his furrowed brow, and his hands clasped tightly together, knuckles turning white.

"The people of the Four Great Families have revolted," Jadyn said before Austyn could ask. "They control the key routes in Mausoleum Rudolf. They're everywhere outside."

Austyn remained silent, simply watching him.

Jadyn, perhaps just looking for someone to talk to, continued, seemingly not expecting a response from Austyn. "The people of the Four Great Families have always resented me. They can't stand us just because we're outsiders who took what they believed was theirs! They're envious. Seeing our power grow, they want to band together and destroy us!"

"Not us," Austyn coldly corrected him. "You."

Jadyn retorted angrily, "In their eyes, you belong to me! If I die, you won't have a good life either! We're in this together, whether you understand it or not!"

"I told you, I'm done with you," Austyn said expressionlessly.

"Junior brother, stop this," Jadyn's voice suddenly softened. He nearly knelt before Austyn, pleading, "I know I was wrong. I shouldn't have treated you that way. Please, for the sake of our years of brotherhood, don't be mad at me anymore. Let's return to Mountain Wenhaver. After this blows over, I'll go wherever you want to travel. I'll be with you, okay?"

Austyn looked at the groveling Jadyn before him, feeling an overwhelming sense of absurdity. He suddenly felt he no longer recognized this person named Jadyn.

"And the people of Mausoleum Rudolf?" Austyn asked softly. "And your subordinates, your soldiers, the conscripted musicians. What about them?"

"What do their lives matter to me?" Jadyn replied without thinking.

Austyn looked at him in disbelief. "Not matter? You're the governor of Mausoleum Rudolf. This is your city. The people and soldiers revere and trust you like a god, yet you don't even dare to fight, abandoning the entire city to escape alone?"

"Not alone," Jadyn gently covered Austyn's hand. "I'll have you, Austyn. Having you by my side is enough."

Austyn was utterly speechless. He looked at Jadyn coldly, smiled dryly, and said nothing more.

The carriage bumped and swayed through the chaotic streets of Mausoleum Rudolf. Along the way, the sounds of shouting and the clash of weapons were incessant. Austyn reached out to lift the curtain, but Jadyn, his face full of fear, grabbed his hand, shaking his head to signal not to lift it. Austyn pushed Jadyn aside disdainfully and carefully lifted the curtain slightly, only to peek out once he confirmed it was safe.

Looking back, Austyn's heart tightened, and he held his breath.

The street behind the carriage was littered with corpses, their attire indicating they were conscripted musicians, death warriors from the Four Great Families, and guards from Shaw Mansion. Their carriage was splattered with blood. The horses galloped madly through the blood-soaked streets, rushing out of the north gate.

"Stop!"

Suddenly, the carriage came to an abrupt halt.

Austyn, unsteady on his feet, fell back onto Jadyn.

"What happened?" Jadyn hastily lifted the curtain and asked the guard driving the carriage.

"Mr. Brown, there are many people ahead!" The guard wiped the cold sweat from his forehead.

"An ambush!?"

Jadyn looked up to see a dense crowd on the road ahead. Soldiers holding torches like swarming fireflies stretched for miles, illuminating the pitch-black wilderness. A tall command flag fluttered in the wind, bearing the large character "Harris."

A handsome man, about forty, rode out from the ranks on a tall horse, looking down at Jadyn with an air of calm nobility.

"Are you the governor of Mausoleum Rudolf, Jadyn?" The man's voice was strong and weathered, like sandpaper.

Jadyn got off the carriage. Faced with such overwhelming military power, he knew he stood no chance, so he forced himself to remain calm, standing tall and addressing the man. "Yes, I am. Who are you? An ally of the rebels in the city?"

The man seemed amused by Jadyn's question and laughed. From behind him came a familiar voice, saying, "He can't even recognize the King's flag and dares to ask if we're rebels."

Austyn, just getting up in the carriage, heard this familiar voice and felt his heart leap into his throat.

He wasn't mistaken. It was Timothy!

Austyn was so overjoyed that his fingers trembled. He could no longer contain himself and eagerly lifted the curtain, peering out.

A man in white armor with a bow on his back rode out of the darkness. In the firelight, his handsome face was striking, a smirk playing at the corners of his lips. It was Timothy.

"Timothy? King of Nixie?" Jadyn muttered in disbelief.

"This man called us rebels, Mr. Shaw," the King of Nixie glanced at Timothy. "What should I do with him?"

"To the victor belongs the spoils," Timothy said calmly. "Only the defeated are called traitors. That's the way it's always been."

Jadyn finally snapped out of it, pointing angrily at Timothy. "Timothy! I, Jadyn, have treated you well all this time. When have I ever wronged you? Why stab me in the back after leaving?"

"Who do you think I'm doing this for?" Timothy smiled slightly, looking at Austyn. "Austyn, I finally found you. Jadyn said you wouldn't come with me. I didn't believe it and wanted to ask you myself."

Austyn's chest tightened. He took a deep breath, his usually calm face flushing slightly.

Timothy removed his white robe and said loudly, "Austyn, I, Timothy, will never force you to do anything against your will. Wherever you want to go, no matter how far, I will accompany you. Wear this white robe, and I'll be with you always."

As a gust of wind blew, Timothy released the white robe, which floated into Austyn's arms. Austyn grasped the still-warm robe tightly. Timothy's words echoed in his heart, stirring strong emotions. His eyes welled up, a tear rolling down his cheek.

Word by word, he declared firmly, "To the ends of the earth, with you."

Jadyn, already in a desperate situation, watched Austyn and Timothy's heartfelt reunion. Rage surged from his feet to his head.

Facing an unwinnable situation and being abandoned by his closest companion of fifteen years, Jadyn's mind was consumed by a whirlwind of humiliation, jealousy, and anger, obliterating any remaining sanity.

With a sudden swoosh, Jadyn pulled out a gleaming dagger from his chest and seized Austyn by the throat from behind, pressing the blade against Austyn's neck.

Timothy was horrified. "Jadyn, what are you trying to do!?"

This move completely took Timothy by surprise. He had thought that Austyn was a valuable pawn for Jadyn and that no matter how desperate Jadyn became, he wouldn't harm his junior brother, Austyn.

But it seemed even a cornered dog would leap over a wall.

Jadyn's dark, lifeless eyes were now brimming with murderous intent.

"Isn't it him you want? Well, I'll make sure you don't get him!" Jadyn sneered, and the dagger in his hand plunged deep into Austyn's delicate skin.

Before anyone could react, a swift arrow whizzed through the night, striking Jadyn's arm. With a scream of pain, Jadyn's grip loosened, and the dagger clattered to the ground.

Austyn jabbed his elbow into Jadyn's chest, seizing the chance to break free and collapsing to the ground.

"Austyn! Get over here!" Timothy shouted, his eyes fixed on Jadyn, quickly drawing another arrow.

"Don't kill him!" Austyn's urgent cry echoed, and almost simultaneously, Timothy released the arrow.

Perhaps influenced by Austyn's shout, the second arrow missed its mark, grazing Jadyn's cheek and leaving a bloody streak.

Timothy clicked his tongue in frustration, readying another arrow, but Jadyn's guards rushed forward, grabbing the bleeding Jadyn and dragging him back to the carriage.

With a sharp neigh, the carriage turned and bolted into the nearby underbrush, disappearing into the night.

Timothy had no time to worry about the fleeing Jadyn. He jumped off his horse and hurried to Austyn's side, helping him up.

"Austyn! Are you alright!?"

"Timothy... I..."

Austyn looked up, and as their eyes met, the tension that had been holding him together finally snapped. On the brink of collapse, he clung to Timothy's hand, barely able to stand.

Seeing that Austyn had no serious injuries, Timothy breathed a sigh of relief. He embraced Austyn, gently stroking his back and soothing him. "It's over. Everything is over now."

Austyn's nose tingled, and unable to hold back any longer, he clung to Timothy's back, tears of pent-up emotion streaming silently down his face.

While Timothy and Austyn were lost in their tearful reunion, the chaos in Mausoleum Rudolf was also nearing its end. Soldiers in armor stormed the now-deserted Shaw Mansion, searching every room as if looking for something.

"Search everywhere! Leave no one alive!"

Penelope stood tall in Shaw Mansion, his ancestral spear in hand. Clad in crimson armor, he cut a striking figure of power and elegance.

To avoid disturbing the citizens of Mausoleum Rudolf, the main force, led by the King of Nixie, had camped outside the city. Penelope, leading a vanguard of elite troops, entered the city to help the Four Great Families mop up the remnants and clear the battlefield.

Now, he was in Shaw Mansion on Timothy's orders to find a particular man.

About the time it takes to burn a stick of incense later, a soldier rushed over, kneeling before Penelope and saluting.

"Mr. Morris, we've searched Shaw Mansion thoroughly and found only one person!"

Two soldiers dragged a man before Penelope and dropped him at his feet.

Penelope crouched down, grasped the man's chin, and studied his features.

The man, unconscious and with his eyes closed, was fair-skinned and handsome.

After Jadyn fled, the staff at Shaw Mansion, knowing disaster was imminent, had scattered—except for Urijah, who had been knocked out by Jadyn.

Penelope didn't know Urijah's name. He only knew that Timothy was looking for someone in Shaw Mansion. He assumed Urijah was the person Timothy wanted, scrutinizing him for a moment before snorting, "I thought he'd be a stunning beauty. Turns out, he's nothing special."

He stood up and waved to his men. "Take this person back to camp. We're leaving."

Chapter Forty-Four: The End of the Line

The upheaval in Mausoleum Rudolf came swiftly and departed just as quickly. Once the flames died down, everything returned to an eerie calm. The King of Nixie led his troops back to the camp outside Mausoleum Rudolf, with Timothy and Austyn riding together on the same horse.

After the ordeal, Austyn was utterly exhausted. Wrapped in a white robe, he leaned quietly against Timothy, feeling an indescribable sense of safety and peace.

"Congratulations, Mr. Shaw, for winning your beauty," the King of Nixie teased.

Timothy gave a bitter smile, thinking about the promise he had made to Austyn. His heart was filled with a mix of emotions. He glanced down to see Austyn's eyelids fluttering as he struggled to stay awake. Finding it amusing, Timothy reached out to tease his eyelashes.

Austyn blinked, feeling ticklish, and opened his eyes. "What are you doing?" he asked, blinking again.

Timothy loved it when Austyn blinked at him like this; it was a rare show of cuteness from someone usually so calm and composed.

"Finally awake?" Timothy smiled. "Is my body that comfortable to sleep on?"

"Yes." Austyn's eyebrows curved as he gave a faint smile. "For some reason, I feel especially secure when I'm with you."

Seeing Austyn's tired face, Timothy knew he hadn't had a good rest during his time under Jadyn's control. He felt a wave of guilt.

"I'm sorry I didn't come sooner. You must have been so scared."

"You had your plans. I always believed you would come."

Timothy's smile was half amused, half serious. "You trust me that much? Or did you calculate it?"

"I didn't need to calculate. I just knew," Austyn said softly. "I believed you would come."

Timothy indeed had his own plans. Since the day he left Rickie, he had never stopped communicating with the King of Nixie. Along the way, Timothy documented everything he saw in Kamal, his experiences in Mausoleum Rudolf, the character of Jadyn, and the internal situation of Mausoleum Rudolf. He sent these reports to the King of Nixie via carrier pigeons.

This included his plan to ally with the Four Great Families.

Originally, Timothy intended to stay in Mausoleum Rudolf for only five or six days. But after learning about Austyn's plight, he changed his mind.

The idea of allying with the Four Great Families arose then.

Luckily, they met Dawsyn, whose support was crucial. With Dawsyn's mediation, Timothy gained the trust of the Four Great Families and turned his plan into reality.

The Sunder soldiers and the Four Great Families launched a surprise attack on Jadyn, catching him off guard.

Honestly, it was a bold plan, almost a gamble. When the King of Nixie first heard of it, he shook his head repeatedly, saying the stakes were too high and the consequences of failure would be severe.

After all, the Four Great Families had no military power and could only rely on their death warriors and government troops. If Jadyn decided to defend Mausoleum Rudolf to the death, it would undoubtedly be a bloody battle.

But as a seasoned gambler, Timothy was resolute. He bet that Jadyn wouldn't dare fight head-on.

Through his observations, Timothy felt he understood Jadyn's character. Jadyn was an empty shell, lacking real substance. Without Mausoleum Rudolf, he could retreat to Mountain Wenhaver, lay low for a year or two, and then resurface elsewhere to continue his deceit.

For someone with no real skills, who could only survive by trickery, fighting to the death for Mausoleum Rudolf was impossible—Timothy gambled on this point.

And the outcome proved Timothy right. Jadyn fled at the first sign of danger, demoralizing his troops. The conscripted musicians scattered like sand, hiding or fleeing. Except for the path of corpses left in Jadyn's wake, the battles in Mausoleum Rudolf ended almost before they began.

Compared to the determined Four Great Families, Jadyn's troops were a disorganized rabble, quickly collapsing in defeat.

Back at camp, Timothy reported the entire incident to the King of Nixie. Late into the night, Timothy finally left the tent, only to see a familiar figure.

Penelope, clad in battle gear with a crimson cloak fluttering in the wind, stood not far away, seemingly waiting for someone.

"Isn't this Mr. Morris? Out for a walk at this hour? Waiting for someone?" Timothy stopped a few steps away from Penelope, eyeing him with a playful smile.

Penelope turned slightly, raising an eyebrow. "Just getting some fresh air, enjoying the view. Do you have a problem with that?"

"No, why would I have a problem?" Timothy glanced at Penelope's dew-soaked cloak, understanding immediately. "I won't stand in the way of your view. It's cold out; be careful not to catch a chill."

Timothy turned to leave but heard Penelope's voice behind him. "Timothy, I was wrong about you."

"What?" Timothy frowned, turning back.

Penelope looked at him with disdain. "I thought you had some taste. I didn't expect you'd be desperate enough to take in that kind of trash."

"What trash?" Timothy was puzzled.

"I brought you the person you wanted, but sharing a room with that kind of person disgusted me. Take him away."

Timothy entered Penelope's tent and saw someone beaten black and blue, cowering in a corner.

"Urijah?"

Timothy was shocked, wondering why Urijah was in Penelope's tent. Then he remembered—he had sent Urijah to Shaw Mansion to find out about Austyn. But with so many things happening, Timothy had completely forgotten about Urijah.

Seeing Timothy, Urijah rushed over like a savior, hugging his waist. "Timothy! You're finally here. Where is this place? Why is everyone here so fierce, especially this guy!"

Hiding behind Timothy, Urijah shot a fearful glance at Penelope.

Timothy looked at Urijah and then at Penelope, curiosity in his eyes. "What did you do to him to scare him like this?"

"What? Feeling sorry for your little lover? Why don't you ask him? I spared his life for your sake. Otherwise..." Penelope sneered, leaving the rest unsaid.

Timothy had a good guess. Urijah must have tried to flirt with Penelope, not realizing he was poking a tiger. Penelope had likely taught him a hard lesson.

The thought was too amusing for Timothy. "Wait, Mr. Morris, you must have misunderstood. He's not my lover. We have no such relationship!"

"Timothy! How can you say that?" Urijah looked up, smearing his tears and snot on Timothy's chest. "I risked my life to save your Austyn."

"Austyn?"

Hearing another unfamiliar name, Penelope's patience wore thin. His face darkened, and his fists clenched.

"This is a long story...!" Timothy was at his wit's end, unsure why he felt the need to explain to Penelope. He only knew Penelope seemed like a volcano ready to erupt, eyes blazing with fury.

Urijah, however, clung to Timothy, pressing his hand to his bruised forehead. "Timothy, feel this. It's bleeding! I nearly lost my life for you. Don't I deserve some credit?"

Penelope finally lost his temper.

"Both of you, get out of here!"

With a deafening roar, Urijah and Timothy were kicked out of the tent.

Timothy was speechless with anger. Nothing good ever happened when he was with Urijah. But since Urijah had helped him, Timothy couldn't just turn his back on him now.

So, Timothy led Urijah back to his tent, feeling utterly defeated. Austyn and Adam were still awake. After Austyn returned to the camp, Adam treated his wounds while explaining the entire situation to him.

In front of Adam, Urijah dared not act up anymore. Instead, he obediently held the bedding Timothy had thrown at him, curling up at the edge of the couch. His well-behaved demeanor was a stark contrast to his previous antics.

"Austyn, what happened to you?" Timothy was startled to see Austyn's neck wrapped in bandages. "Are you hurt?"

Austyn touched the back of his neck and shook his head lightly. "I just got a minor scratch during the standoff outside the city. It's nothing serious. If it weren't for Mr. Garcia noticing, I wouldn't have realized it myself."

As Adam cleaned up the medicinal residues and bandages, he said, "We who roam the martial world are used to it, but Master

Powell, with your delicate skin, even minor injuries should not be taken lightly."

"Mr. Garcia deserves the credit," Austyn said admiringly. "When it comes to meticulousness, I must concede defeat."

Timothy felt proud as Austyn praised Adam, hugging Adam's shoulder with a laugh. "Of course, our Adam is not only meticulous but also very caring."

Adam blushed, nudging Timothy in the waist with his fist. "What do you mean by 'our'? Besides, Master Powell praised me, what are you getting so proud of?"

Austyn smiled slightly. "Mr. Garcia, you, I really appreciate what you've done for me. Without you, I can't imagine what would have happened to me..."

"Yes, but it's all over now. From today on, you are a free man. You can return to Mountain Wenhaver or go anywhere you wish. From now on, you don't need to worry about being controlled by anyone," Timothy said with emotion.

Austyn's lowered eyelids trembled slightly. "Can I really go anywhere I want?"

"Of course. Tell me, where do you want to go?" Timothy asked.

Austyn was silent for a long time. Finally, he raised his head and looked quietly at Timothy. "I want to stay by your side."

At these words, both Timothy and Adam were taken aback.

In the flickering candlelight, Austyn's eyes glimmered with a faint, hazy light as he looked at Timothy.

Timothy was speechless, and it was Adam who gently poked Timothy in the waist, snapping him out of his stupor.

"I..." Timothy suddenly felt parched. He opened his mouth, trying to find the right words, but Austyn spoke again.

"You broke my fate, led me out of my current predicament, and gave me a chance to start anew. I want to repay you. Although I am insignificant and weak, if you don't mind, I would like to go to Poiema with you and lend you a hand."

"Oh...that's what you meant. I thought..." Timothy laughed sheepishly, scratching his warm cheek with a finger.

Austyn raised an eyebrow and blinked. "Thought what?"

"Nothing! Nothing!" To ease the awkward atmosphere, Timothy let out a dry laugh.

Of course, Timothy also wanted to return to Poiema immediately, but he couldn't just leave because Jadyn had left a mess behind. When the news of Jadyn's flight spread, rumors began circulating in the city: Jadyn hadn't fled but had ascended to immortality. Some fanatical followers fled with their families, and some even drowned themselves, swearing to follow Jadyn in death. Mausoleum Rudolf was in chaos, with people in panic.

To calm the public, people from the Four Great Families approached Timothy, suggesting that Austyn personally explain to the people how Jadyn had deceived them.

Timothy was unsure. While this might stabilize the situation, it would also push Austyn into the spotlight. Austyn had just escaped one pit, and Timothy couldn't bear to push him into another.

Surprisingly, Austyn agreed to the Four Great Families' proposal. Timothy urged him to reconsider, as Mausoleum Rudolf was a quagmire that would be hard to escape from. However, Austyn believed that since his senior brother was gone, it was reasonable for him to resolve the issue.

Seeing that Austyn had made up his mind, Timothy had no more to say.

The date was set for three days later. At Temple Kalpana, a grand ceremony would be held, and Austyn, invited by the Four Great Families, would preside over the ceremony and reveal the truth to the city.

The day before the ceremony, Austyn suddenly proposed going for a walk, saying he had never properly appreciated the city. Timothy readily agreed and accompanied Austyn on a leisurely stroll through the city. They ate at a century-old shop in the north and visited the market in the south. They walked from the east to the west of the city, finally climbing the walls of Mausoleum Rudolf as the sun set, painting the sky with hues of orange.

Timothy and Austyn stood side by side on the city wall. Mausoleum Rudolf had regained its peace and order from the chaos of the previous days, presenting a serene and harmonious scene.

However, Timothy's gaze was more often on the person beside him than on the city.

Austyn was undeniably beautiful. He had a high, straight nose, and his long lashes fluttered. The breeze occasionally lifted a strand of his hair, and the glow of the sunset in his clear eyes revealed a touch of loneliness.

"Sorry, this time, I might have to go back on my word."

"Hmm? What did you say?" Timothy, lost in his thoughts as he stared at Austyn's profile, asked in confusion.

Austyn remained silent for a long time, then spoke with determination. "The people from the Four Great Families told me they don't want me to leave Mausoleum Rudolf."

Timothy was stunned for a moment before he realized what was being said. "Why? Didn't you agree to explain the situation to the people?"

"They fear that if I leave, Mausoleum Rudolf will fall into chaos, so they hope I will stay and take charge."

Timothy's mind exploded. "What? Does that mean you have to stay here for life!?"

"They said it's only temporary. Once Mausoleum Rudolf is stable, they won't interfere with wherever I go."

"No! I don't agree!" Timothy declared firmly. "I did all this to ensure you wouldn't be controlled by anyone anymore. Now that Jadyn is gone, and the Four Great Families are here, it means all my efforts were in vain. I didn't help you at all!"

"No, you've helped me a lot," Austyn shook his head. "Without you, I might never have escaped my senior brother's control, forever his puppet. Now, I am free...but I can't abandon this city irresponsibly like my senior brother did."

Turning to Timothy, Austyn's gaze was firm. "Trust me, this time, I will handle everything."

Timothy was silent for a long time, looking at Austyn with a forlorn expression. "For the first time, I feel that being too responsible isn't always a good thing." He sighed deeply. "Forget it. Ultimately, it's my fault. I wanted to give you freedom, but I ended up binding you."

"You're wrong. I was already trapped long ago." Austyn rested his head on Timothy's shoulder. "Do you remember what I promised you?"

"Of course I do." Timothy gently hugged Austyn's waist. "You promised to pretend to fall in love with me, to elope with me, to put on a show for Jadyn."

Austyn said softly, "Now that the play is over, it's time for the final curtain, but I've become so engrossed in the act that I can't get out."

Timothy's chest tightened, his heart racing.

Austyn lifted his gaze, looking intently at Timothy. "It's not Mausoleum Rudolf that binds me; it's you."

In the setting sun, Austyn's face was flushed, his eyes bright and full of emotion.

Timothy felt his mouth go dry, his breath quickening.

"Just indulge my whim," Austyn whispered dreamily. "Will you accompany me to finish this last act?"

Timothy's emotions surged. Without answering, he found himself holding Austyn's waist and kissing those lips that had spoken a whimsical wish.

That kiss stirred a pond of spring water by the wind. At first, their lips and tongues only lightly and tentatively explored each other, until Timothy finally captured Austyn's shy tongue tip, gently entwining it with his own, filled with tender affection. Perhaps due to the reluctance and helplessness of their impending separation, the extreme tenderness was laced with a hint of sorrow and bitterness. Timothy sucked deeply and slowly, while Austyn wrapped his arms around Timothy's neck, moving provocatively, almost sacrificially, until the entwined saliva carried a bittersweet taste.

When the kiss ended and their lips parted, both were breathless. Timothy's groin was swollen and painful, pressing hard against Austyn's abdomen. Austyn's face was flushed, his moist, red lips slightly parted, seemingly and unintentionally tempting Timothy.

"What do you want me to do next?" Timothy swallowed, asking softly.

Austyn, still clinging to Timothy's neck, whispered in his ear, "Make me yours, inside and out, completely."

Austyn's words ignited the suppressed desire in Timothy's heart. Their lips met again, no longer tender but fiercely entwined, with silvery threads of saliva occasionally catching the light, adding a provocative and lascivious sheen. While kissing, Timothy's hand moved down quickly, untying Austyn's belt and pulling off his underpants.

"Hmm...!"

Halfway through the kiss, Austyn's body was lifted into the air, sitting on a recess of the city wall. Timothy bent down, taking Austyn's flaccid member into his mouth, sucking eagerly.

"We'll be...seen!" Austyn, fearing to fall, clung tightly to the wall with one hand, while nervously holding Timothy's head with the other. His legs gradually spread open before Timothy.

Austyn's protests were soon drowned in the wet sounds of Timothy's sucking. His member, sensitive to teasing, quickly became erect under Timothy's ministrations, oozing with pleasure. The sticky fluid flowed down the stiff shaft, moistening the tight entrance.

Timothy's fingers followed suit, dipping into the slick nectar, parting the shyly closed flesh, probing into the hidden place.

In the dim twilight, in the deserted corners of the city wall, Austyn's legs were spread wide, while Timothy's head moved up and down between them. Austyn raised his hand, biting down on his wrist, his waist shivering uncontrollably, his lower abdomen convulsing in waves.

After Timothy had thoroughly licked and teased Austyn, he finally stood up, unbuckling his belt. Austyn watched wide-eyed as Timothy's erect member sprang out, gulping involuntarily.

"So big, will it fit?"

Compared to Timothy's large endowment, his own seemed quite modest.

"Leave it to me." Timothy grabbed Austyn's hand, making him cling tightly to his neck. Then, guiding his member, he slowly pushed it into the moist entrance.

"Ah...!"

As the thick shaft gradually penetrated, Austyn winced, letting out a low gasp, instinctively tightening his hold on Timothy's neck. Despite being mentally prepared and Timothy's gentleness, the pain of being torn open made Austyn acutely aware of being possessed by Timothy.

Though painful, it was more thrilling, joyous, and satisfying.

Desiring to become Timothy's, wanting him to go deeper, Austyn unconsciously lifted his hips, welcoming Timothy in.

Despite Austyn's active participation, Timothy didn't want to hurt him. Knowing it was Austyn's first time, he started slowly, only entering halfway, moving gently with shallow thrusts.

"Does it still hurt?" Timothy asked, kissing Austyn's eyes, rubbing his waist tenderly.

Austyn moaned softly, "Even if it hurts, it's you, and I like it."

Timothy took a sharp breath, feeling his desire swell further, pressing deeper unintentionally.

"If you keep saying things like that, I won't be able to hold back."

"Why hold back?" Austyn's eyes were seductive. "Do whatever you want; I can take it."

"This is what you said!"

Austyn's words unlocked something in Timothy. He stopped holding back, lifting Austyn entirely and thrusting upwards forcefully.

"Ah!"

With a broken cry, the thick shaft plunged to the deepest point.

Held tightly in Timothy's strong arms, Austyn had no control over his body, only moving up and down with Timothy's rhythm, each thrust hitting his sensitive spots, sending waves of pleasure through him.

The position was so deep, Austyn feared Timothy's shaft might reach his throat. He clung desperately to Timothy's waist, the weapon in his burning passage driving in and out relentlessly.

Austyn lost track of when he climaxed, only knowing that when he came to, his abdomen was slick with wetness, having unknowingly released himself.

Timothy, with his impressive strength, held Austyn and thrust several hundred times before finally shuddering, shooting his essence deep into Austyn. The sensation of being filled made Austyn's scalp tingle, and a tear slipped silently from his eye.

When Timothy's member finally slid out, leaving a trail of sticky white fluid, both were far from satisfied. Timothy turned Austyn around, pressing him against the wall. Austyn eagerly complied, presenting his hips openly. Seeing the yearning entrance oozing white foam, Timothy couldn't hold back, plunging back in.

This time, entering from behind, Timothy started with deep, vigorous thrusts, making the wet sounds louder, fluids splashing everywhere.

In this storm of passion, Austyn could only gasp and moan. Without Timothy's support, his trembling legs wouldn't have held him up.

Timothy wrapped an arm around Austyn's upper body, kissing him deeply to stifle his moans. Austyn whimpered, twisting and arching to meet Timothy's thrusts, eagerly entwining their tongues in passionate kisses.

They kissed until they nearly suffocated, then resumed their feverish coupling.

Austyn gripped the wall tightly, his nails digging into the stone, while Timothy held his arm from behind, thrusting relentlessly. Sweat glistened on their foreheads, dripping onto their entwined bodies.

Timothy, seemingly tireless, drove into Austyn's swollen passage repeatedly, filling him with his desire. Only when night fell and both were utterly exhausted did Timothy finally relent.

Under a sky full of stars, Timothy and Austyn sat in a corner of the wall, foreheads touching, breathing heavily.

The night was beautiful and quiet.

Reluctant to break the rare peace, they gazed at each other in silent understanding, sharing a knowing smile.

Timothy, utterly spent, collapsed softly into Austyn's embrace.

Austyn tenderly caressed Timothy's roguish brows, smiling gently, his eyes filled with warmth.

Chapter Forty-Five: Defense Through Offense

The next day, under the watchful eyes of the masses, Austyn, dressed in a magnificent ceremonial robe, ascended the altar. Amidst the sea of people, with their gazes filled with suspicion, anxiety, anticipation, and prayers, he stood alone, dignified and poised, his every movement exuding calmness and composure.

For many years, he had been like an elusive shadow, silently contributing everything he had to the city from behind Jadyn. Now, he had merely stepped out from the shadows into the sunlight, and his actions remained unchanged.

Not only the citizens of Mausoleum Rudolf but also the Four Great Families, and even Timothy, were deeply drawn, impressed, and moved by Austyn's resolute demeanor.

Timothy stood among the crowd, watching from a distance as Austyn performed fluid and graceful movements on the altar, witnessing the citizens kneel in waves at Austyn's feet, tears of gratitude streaming down their faces. Everything seemed peaceful and settled, a happy ending. Yet, Timothy couldn't help but feel a faint bitterness in his heart.

With a sigh, Timothy quietly turned to leave.

This time, Timothy left with the King of Nixie and Penelope's group. Before departing, Adam visited Dawsyn's home, where the old and young held each other's hands, seemingly having endless words to say. It was said that Dawsyn had adopted Adam as a godson, and Timothy was genuinely happy for Adam.

As for Urijah, he stood beside Julia, winking at Timothy, saying, "Timothy, don't forget me, Urijah, when you hit it big!" which earned him a roll of the eyes from Penelope, who teased Timothy, "You even go after married men." Timothy could only smile helplessly, too lazy to explain. Penelope already regarded him as a hopeless case, so no amount of explanation would change her mind. He didn't mind letting himself appear worse.

As they exited the gates of Mausoleum Rudolf, they suddenly heard a flute playing behind them. Timothy felt a tug at his heart and reined in his horse to look back, spotting a lone figure standing on the city wall.

The attire, the style, and the flute music unmistakably identified Austyn.

Timothy stopped, gazing at the distant figure with a growing sense of sadness.

"Was it him you wanted me to find at Shaw Mansion?" Penelope, who had unknowingly ridden up beside him, asked suddenly.

"Yes." Timothy nodded, his eyes still fixed on the figure.

Penelope pressed her lips together, saying nothing. She looked at Timothy's profile, then at the figure on the wall.

"I take back what I said. Your taste isn't bad after all," Penelope huffed. "Though still not quite as good as mine."

Timothy couldn't help but laugh. The bitterness that had been gnawing at him these past days was swept away by Penelope's jest. He turned to retort, but Penelope gave him no chance, riding off in a cloud of dust.

When Timothy turned back, the figure on the wall had vanished, and even the flute music had faded away, as if it had all been just a dream.

Compared to Austyn, Jadyn's fate was far worse.

The day he escaped Mausoleum Rudolf, Jadyn, escorted by two guards, fled westward into Poiema.

Now, Jadyn had nothing. He had no power or influence, and without Austyn, he had no significant skills, save for his eloquence.

Unwilling to accept his defeat, Jadyn decided to enter the palace to present a memorial to Queen Owen, accusing Timothy and the King of Nixie of collusion and rebellion.

To achieve this, Jadyn sold almost all his remaining possessions, bribing palace guards, eunuchs, and maids. He staked everything on this final desperate gamble.

On this day, Jadyn instructed his two bodyguards to wait outside the palace for his signal. Carrying the memorial he had written overnight, he entered the palace.

Having already arranged everything, Jadyn made his way unimpeded to the forbidden garden.

According to his informant, Queen Owen would be watching a performance there today.

As he approached the stage, he heard the sound of flutes and strings. The stage, draped in red curtains, featured performers in colorful, embroidered costumes singing in high-pitched voices.

However, to Jadyn's surprise, it was not Queen Owen in the audience, but the emperor, Christopher.

Fate had not favored him. Queen Owen had left due to illness, leaving him with a difficult choice. He could abandon his plan and return another day, losing all the money he had spent to get this far, or proceed, risking everything.

Biting his lip, Jadyn made the fateful decision, presenting his memorial to Christopher.

At that moment, Jadyn did not know the relationship between Christopher and Timothy. Had he known, he would never have made this choice.

Christopher took the memorial, his face darkening as he read.

Jadyn, seeing Christopher's reaction, was overjoyed, believing it to be the emperor's expected response to learning of his subjects' rebellion.

Christopher quickly regained his composure, putting the memorial aside. He halted the performance, dismissed the palace maids and eunuchs, leaving only a guard by his side.

Once alone, he signaled for Jadyn to rise.

Jadyn stood, awaiting further instruction.

Christopher, clutching the memorial, paced for a moment before turning back to Jadyn.

"What do you suggest I do?" he asked.

Jadyn, suppressing his excitement, declared, "Issue a decree immediately, stripping Timothy and the King of Nixie of their military power, and proclaim their crimes to rally the states and counties to rise against the rebels!"

Christopher stared at Jadyn, taking a deep breath. "Very well, I will issue the decree. But first, I need to borrow something from you."

Jadyn was confused. "What does Your Majesty wish to borrow?" Before he could react, he felt a sharp pain in his abdomen.

Christopher released the sword hilt, the blade—meant for the guard—now embedded in Jadyn's stomach, staining his clothes dark red.

The guard quickly stepped forward to catch Jadyn as he collapsed, eyes wide in disbelief.

"Take him away and deal with the body," Christopher ordered, not meeting Jadyn's eyes.

The guard obeyed, carrying Jadyn's lifeless body away.

Christopher looked at his bloodstained hand, trembling and unable to calm down.

A crash interrupted his thoughts. A vase had shattered on the floor.

Austyn instinctively bent to pick it up, cutting his finger on the sharp shards. He gasped softly, watching a drop of blood form before quickly sucking on his finger.

Somehow, he felt restless and uneasy today, as if something significant was about to happen.

"Junior Brother..."

A familiar voice suddenly rang in Austyn's ears, startling him into a cold sweat. He turned around, looking everywhere, but the room was empty, with no trace of his senior brother, Jadyn.

Am I losing my mind?

Austyn clutched his rapidly beating chest, breathing heavily. After calming himself down, he opened the door and stepped out of Qingchuan Residence. It was already late at night. He looked up at the star-filled sky, pinched his fingers together, and calculated something silently. Suddenly, he trembled all over, his face turning pale.

He immediately turned back to his room, went to his desk, spread out some letter paper, and dipped his pen in ink. Under the flickering candlelight, his solitary figure was left writing urgently by the window.

The written letter was sealed and handed to a messenger who quickly left Mausoleum Rudolf. Within a day, the letter was in Timothy's hands.

When Timothy received Austyn's letter, he was in the King of Nixie's tent, discussing the route of their advance with Penelope. He took the letter and read it, his brows furrowing.

"What's wrong?" Adam asked curiously, noticing Timothy's grim expression. "Whose letter is it?"

"It's from Austyn," Timothy said solemnly. "He says that Jadyn might have met with misfortune."

"Oh..." Adam seemed indifferent upon hearing this. "What does it have to do with you? Why the long face?"

"Austyn says he observed the stars and predicted that there will be changes in the palace within a few days."

The King of Nixie's expression changed. "Could something have happened to the Emperor?"

"Your Highness need not worry," Penelope said calmly. "Since it says 'within a few days,' it means the Emperor is safe for now."

"But how many days are 'a few days'? Ten days are 'a few days,' and so are two days," Adam murmured. "What if it's the latter? The front is Gaylord. From Gaylord to Poiema, even at a fast march, it will take five days. If something happens in Poiema within those five days, what do we do then?"

Adam's words cast a heavy silence over everyone, and the atmosphere became tense.

After a long silence, Timothy spoke, "It seems we have to take the initiative."

Penelope asked, "What do you mean by taking the initiative?"

Timothy replied, "We attack Gaylord."

The King of Nixie was shocked and quickly grabbed Timothy's hand. "Absolutely not! Attacking Gaylord now would be equivalent to declaring rebellion and alerting the enemy!"

"That's exactly what I want to do. By alarming the enemy, the Emperor will be safer."

"Why?" Both the King of Nixie and Adam looked at Timothy in confusion.

Timothy winked slyly. "Think about it. If we attack Gaylord under the pretense of purging the traitors, would those led by Queen Owen and Bowie dare to harm the Emperor? That would be tantamount to admitting their disloyalty and giving us a justified reason to eliminate them."

The King of Nixie finally understood, slapping his thigh. "I see! If they want to destroy us, they must first control the Emperor to command the states and counties to send troops against us. So not only will they not harm the Emperor, but they will also show loyalty to prove their innocence!"

"Brilliant strategy," Penelope said, staring at Timothy with a cold hum. "Mr. Shaw, to divert the court's attention, you're willing to make us targets?"

"As long as we can ensure the Emperor's safety, being targets is a small price to pay."

Timothy smiled calmly, full of confidence. Penelope didn't expect Timothy to have such resolve and was left speechless for a moment.

Once the plan was settled, everyone pledged allegiance to the King of Nixie as their commander. Penelope drafted the proclamation and letter of persuasion. The next morning, Timothy, Penelope, and Adam each led twenty thousand troops to attack Gaylord. Timothy rode to the city walls, nocked an arrow, and shot the proclamation into the city. The guards inside picked it up and delivered it to the prefect of Gaylord, Holy Lee.

Holy, Bowie's uncle, was shocked to learn that the King of Nixie was attacking under the pretense of purging traitors. Being a loyal follower of Bowie, he had no intention of surrendering and immediately sent a message to Bowie in Poiema while hastily preparing his troops for battle.

Holy himself climbed the city wall to oversee the battle.

From his vantage point, he saw the King of Nixie's army advancing fiercely. Penelope, wearing a phoenix-feathered helmet and wielding a red-tasseled spear, charged forward in silver armor. Her family's ancestral spear techniques were unstoppable, killing an enemy general within dozens of rounds. Holy sent out three more generals, but all met the same fate, their heads soon piled before Holy, who paled and ordered the gates to be shut tight.

At the King of Nixie's command, sixty thousand troops, led by Penelope, Timothy, and Adam, surged towards the city gates, setting up ladders and catapults to begin the assault.

While the King of Nixie's forces attacked Gaylord, Christopher knelt quietly in prayer at the Temple Lrisa in the forbidden garden of Poiema, hands clasped, murmuring.

Today was the fifth day of the month, his usual day for spiritual reflection. Although Poiema seemed peaceful recently, Christopher felt uneasy, unable to sleep soundly. He sensed that the tranquility was only superficial, hiding an ominous undercurrent.

Having dealt with Jadyn, Christopher thought he had covered all his tracks, but the fear of missing something gnawed at him. What if he had overlooked a detail? What if Jadyn had made other arrangements?

These thoughts kept him anxious and sleepless. He felt the palace's grandeur weighing heavily on him, suffocating him.

He didn't even know how he had survived the past twenty years in this palace without Timothy.

After all these years, Christopher finally decided he couldn't endure it any longer. To change his fate, he needed to take a crucial step.

"Your Majesty," Arya's voice came from behind him. "The person is here."

"Is that so..." Christopher took a deep breath. "Let her in."

Moments later, Arya brought in a woman in her thirties, carrying a small box. She approached silently. Christopher glanced at her, noting her delicate features and respectful demeanor. She didn't speak, only bowing deeply and gesturing.

She appeared to be mute.

"Arya," Christopher turned to Arya, his voice low. "I'm sorry."

Arya responded calmly, "I serve without regret, Your Majesty. No need to apologize."

Christopher nodded and then addressed the woman. "Let's begin."

Chapter Forty-Six: Long-Awaited Reunion

Gaylord was a tough nut to crack. Despite the defending force being only thirty thousand strong, it was more difficult than Timothy had imagined.

It was widely known that the most formidable fighters among the Sunder soldiers were the Nuri warriors. They were a group of scattered fighters, renowned for their excellent horsemanship and fierce combat skills. When Abbe was still around, he often led the Nuri soldiers on swift, agile guerrilla warfare.

However, even the bravest cavalry, including the elite Nuri warriors, found themselves powerless before the tall and sturdy city walls.

For three days, despite King of Nixie's army of sixty thousand relentlessly attacking, they failed to take Gaylord. Not only were they repeatedly repelled, suffering heavy losses, but even Timothy himself narrowly escaped an assassination attempt.

Timothy was commanding the siege when suddenly an arrow came flying straight at him. Reflexively raising his hand, he blocked it with a jade ring on his thumb, which shattered with a resounding clang.

Abbe had once said that he gave Timothy the jade ring to protect him. To Timothy's surprise, the ring did exactly that, blocking the fatal arrow and saving his life.

Timothy shuddered to think of the consequences had it not been for that ring.

Even more unfortunate was that half of the shattered jade ring fell to the ground and was buried in the dust. Amidst the chaos,

Timothy didn't have the chance to dismount and search for it. After the battle, Timothy returned to the battlefield alone, but no matter how hard he looked, he couldn't find the missing half. Though it would be difficult to restore the ring even if found, it was Abbe's only keepsake for Timothy, holding immense sentimental value.

As Timothy walked back to the camp, a mournful owl's hoot echoed from the treetops, mocking his fruitless search and weighing down his steps with melancholy.

Was this fate? Timothy stared at the half ring in his hand, his heart heavy with an inexplicable sorrow.

A broken mirror could be mended, but could this half ring ever find its other half in the vast world?

Lost in thought, Timothy suddenly heard a whoosh as the owl swooped down, snatching the half ring from his hand before flying away.

"My ring!!"

Timothy was startled, quickly mounting his horse to chase the owl. The owl flew like a phantom, its speed unmatched. Frustrated and angry, Timothy shot several arrows at it, but the night was too dark, and the owl too agile, causing all his shots to miss.

After pursuing the owl for miles, sweating profusely, Timothy finally sensed something was amiss. He reined in his horse, cautiously observing his surroundings, noticing a light in the distance that seemed to be a camp. The owl perched on a tree near the camp.

"Finally stopped." Timothy notched an arrow, aiming at the culprit, "I'll shoot you down, you beast."

"Don't hurt him!"

A clear voice suddenly rang out. Timothy froze, his hands paralyzed.

A figure emerged silently from the darkness, wearing a sleek black outfit, standing quietly under the tree. The owl circled him before landing gently on his hand.

"Abbe...?"

Timothy stood stunned for a moment before dismounting, slowly approaching the figure. He could hardly believe his eyes, fearing it was an illusion.

The dappled shadows fell on the familiar face, the dark eyes deep as the night.

"Abbe! It's really you!" Timothy's eyes welled up, as he embraced Abbe tightly. "Why did you leave without a word? Where have you been all this time? Are you well? Have you been eating properly?"

Timothy's joy overflowed, not caring if Abbe could respond, he poured out his heart.

"Idiot!"

Abbe kicked Timothy in the leg, causing him to release his grip, gasping in pain.

"Were you trying to strangle me!?" Abbe glared, tossing something at Timothy. "I came to return this."

Timothy caught it, realizing it was the other half of the ring!

The piece he had desperately sought was in Abbe's possession all along.

"Wait!" Timothy's mind raced, "If you had this half, it means you were on the battlefield then!? You've been around me all along, haven't you!?"

Abbe's eyes flickered, quickly turning away.

"If you don't want to say, I won't force you." Timothy sighed, lowering his gaze. "I won't push you. You can go wherever you want."

Abbe remained silent.

Timothy sighed deeply, spreading his hands. "If you hate me, that's fine. You can stay away from me. But..." he paused, speaking softly, "at least on the battlefield, stay where I can see you, like... the old days."

"The past?" Abbe muttered, "It's gone. Like the dead can't come back to life. A broken ring won't be whole again. The me of today is not the me of yesterday."

Timothy looked at Abbe's sorrowful face, his heart aching. The warm boy he knew seemed lost forever.

"Instead of looking back, look ahead." Abbe pointed to the distant light, "Do you know what that is?"

Still lost in his sorrow, Timothy barely responded, "What did you say?"

Frustrated, Abbe slapped Timothy's back hard.

"That's a granary!"

Timothy yelped, clutching his chest. But Abbe's slap cleared his mind.

"A granary?" Timothy realized, "Could it be Gaylord's?"

"Exactly." Abbe raised an eyebrow, "Strike the enemy's heart, and victory will follow."

Enlightened by Abbe's words, Timothy's eyes brightened.

"I get it! I know what to do! You're a master, always guiding me!"

"I've said all I need to. Now get lost!" Abbe turned to leave.

Timothy grabbed his hand, "You're not coming back with me?"

"Back with you?" Abbe sneered, "I might kill Penelope and ruin your plans."

"If you don't come back, where will you go? With your temper, you won't stay far. You might be among the Sunder soldiers, living in the camp. Or will you stay here?" Timothy looked around, "It's dangerous here. Wolves are howling. What if a wolf eats you?"

Embarrassed, Abbe snapped, "I hate your arrogance! I'd rather be eaten by wolves than go back with you!"

Before he could finish, Timothy hoisted him over his shoulder.

"Idiot! Put me down!" Abbe struggled and shouted, pounding Timothy's back.

"I won't, unless you stop yelling and come back quietly. Or I'll carry you all the way to camp."

Pulling the horse's reins, Timothy turned around and started walking back.

Abbe's face turned beet red. Seeing that Timothy was serious and not just playing around, he became furious, his eyes welling up with tears.

"You said you wouldn't force me, and that I could go wherever I wanted. You're a liar! A big liar!"

"I changed my mind," Timothy replied nonchalantly. "You taught me that one shouldn't always dwell on the past. The me of a moment ago is not the me of now."

"You...!" Abbe was at his wit's end, unable to counter Timothy's quick adaptation. He had no choice but to compromise. "Fine, I agree. Put me down first."

"Agree to what?"

"I agree not to run away or cause trouble."

"That's better." Timothy finally let Abbe down, wrapped an arm around his waist, and whispered in his ear, "Get on the horse."

Abbe, having no escape, reluctantly climbed onto the horse. Timothy mounted after him, holding Abbe close as he took the reins.

Having reunited with Abbe after a long time and finally convincing him to return to the camp, Timothy, now holding the person he had longed for so dearly, couldn't bear to rush. He gently nudged the horse forward, moving slowly.

The journey back was arduous, not because of the difficult path, but because their chests were pressed together. Despite the thick clothing between them, they couldn't avoid a certain degree of friction. Timothy's arousal was evident, pressing against Abbe the whole way. Abbe, aware of this, blushed deeply, his ears burning in the night. Though they remained silent, both were filled with a suppressed desire, ready to ignite at the slightest provocation.

Fortunately, they encountered no one along the way. By the time they returned to the camp, it was already late, and everyone had retired for the night. After dismounting, Timothy led Abbe into the tent, immediately embracing and kissing him.

Abbe initially resisted, but as Timothy's lips and tongue teased him, his body gradually softened. When Timothy's hand reached between his legs, rubbing vigorously through the fabric, Abbe trembled, losing his composure, and returned the kiss passionately.

Fearing that Abbe might escape, Timothy carried him to the bed, hastily pulling at his clothes, eager to touch the private place he hadn't caressed in a long time.

"You scoundrel!" Abbe gasped, glaring at Timothy with a mixture of anger and lust. "Did you bring me back just for this?"

"You said you wanted to be eaten by wolves." Timothy smirked, his fingers probing into Abbe, spreading the tender flesh. "Well, I'm that wolf."

Timothy's shamelessness infuriated Abbe. "You're a beast! Mm...!"

Before Abbe could finish his sentence, Timothy tore open his shirt, exposing his firm chest and sensitive nipples, which Timothy immediately began to suck.

Despite the late hour and the fear of being overheard, Abbe had to cover his mouth to stifle any sound. The tent was filled with the wet sounds of Timothy's sucking, adding to Abbe's shame.

"Hurry up if you're going to do it," Abbe muttered, knowing there was no escape. "Finish quickly."

Timothy, already on edge, took Abbe's words as permission, quickly undoing his belt and positioning himself between Abbe's legs, entering him with ease.

Abbe groaned as Timothy penetrated him, turning his face away, unable to meet Timothy's eyes. He was soon pinned to the bed, being thoroughly taken. With no escape, Abbe could only submit to Timothy's relentless thrusting, feeling the hardness inside him moving in and out.

Despite not being the first time, Abbe's body quickly responded, becoming slick and wet, soft sounds filling the tent. The intimate sounds of their coupling grew louder, adding to the heated atmosphere.

Timothy held Abbe tightly, moving steadily until they both climaxed. Not satisfied, he flipped Abbe over, entering him from behind and continuing. Abbe, arching his back in response, was helpless under Timothy's vigorous thrusts. His own arousal dripped steadily, adding to the sounds of their passion.

The night was long, and Timothy, true to his word, devoured Abbe thoroughly, inside and out. Yet, mindful of the battles ahead, he kept some strength, finishing quickly and holding Abbe close as they slept.

Despite his sometimes shameless behavior, Timothy's embrace was a warm, secure haven. In his arms, Abbe slept deeply and peacefully.

No dreams disturbed their sleep. When Abbe opened his eyes, the daylight was already bright.

Timothy had dressed in his striking uniform, his face glowing with energy. The previous night had rejuvenated him, and he looked ready for the day ahead.

Abbe, on the other hand, felt far from refreshed. His body ached, his waist in particular felt as though it might break, and his lower body was especially sore.

Seeing the stark contrast, Timothy showed a rare moment of consideration, tending to Abbe's needs. He brought warm porridge and insisted on feeding Abbe himself, though Abbe, uncomfortable with Timothy's doting, took the bowl to eat on his own. Timothy, undeterred, stayed close, occasionally touching Abbe, almost like an affectionate dog.

Time flew by, and soon the camp was bustling with activity. Timothy, reluctant to leave, said, "Abbe, I have to go. Rest well today." Abbe glanced at him, remaining silent.

"Don't disappear without a word again. I can't fight if I'm worried about you."

"I'm not a child," Abbe retorted angrily. "I know what to do without your instructions."

"You're right. I was overthinking." Timothy sighed in relief, smiling as he leaned in for a brief kiss. "Wait for me, Abbe."

The kiss was casual yet seemed perfectly natural, leaving Abbe no time to react before Timothy walked out of the tent.

"Timothy!" Abbe called, lifting the tent flap to watch him.

After a moment's hesitation, Abbe softly said, "Don't die."

Though quiet, Timothy heard every word. He paused, then smiled brightly, waving back at Abbe.

Abbe watched Timothy's figure fade into the distance, feeling the lingering warmth on his lips. His heart swelled with emotions, standing there long after Timothy had gone.

Chapter Forty-Seven: Fortunate Missteps

The information provided by Abbe was of great help to Timothy and his troops.

This time, Timothy advised the King of Nixie to lead an elite force to raid the Gaylord granary, luring the Gaylord governor, Holy, out of the city to rescue it, and then ambush him on a narrow path, trapping him like a fish in a barrel.

Shortly after the battle began, Holy received reports from scouts that a detachment from the King of Nixie's army was taking a shortcut straight to the granary outside Gaylord. Hearing this, Holy could no longer sit still and immediately led his troops out of the city, chasing after Timothy towards the granary.

As expected, Holy was ambushed by Penelope halfway.

Caught between Penelope and Timothy, Holy was quickly captured and, with no other option, surrendered the city.

After three days and nights of fierce fighting, Gaylord was captured easily.

Upon entering the city, the King of Nixie immediately organized the troops, ordered them not to disturb the people, and reassured the populace. Those who donated cattle and wine to support the troops were rewarded with gold and silk, quickly stabilizing the people's hearts.

In addition, Timothy posted Penelope's proclamations everywhere, using his eloquence to vividly expose the evil deeds of Bowie Queen Owen's faction, who showed no respect for the king and father, deceived and oppressed the people, and brought disaster to the country. Holy, being Bowie's uncle, was also involved in various shady deals with Bowie, all of which were re-vealed to the public, becoming the hottest topic among the citi-zens of Gaylord.

Of course, the news of Timothy and his men raising an army soon reached Poiema, the capital of Great Alvah.

"Bowie has declared us rebels and ordered the states and counties to send troops to suppress us. As for the emperor, it's said he has been confined in Hall Zona, with Queen Owen solely in charge of the court."

The King of Nixie sighed deeply after reading the military report from the scouts. Despite everything proceeding according to plan, his face was full of worry.

Seeing the familiar side profile that closely resembled Christo-pher's, Timothy was moved. "Is Your Highness still harboring doubts?"

"I'm not worried about the emperor's safety right now. I'm more concerned that if the emperor remains in their hands, it will put us at a disadvantage."

"I understand. So we must act quickly and not give Bowie a chance to mobilize troops. If forces from various places enter the capital and surround us, winning will become even harder."

As they spoke, the sound of clashing weapons and the noise of a fierce fight erupted outside.

Timothy and the King of Nixie stepped out of the tent to see two figures locked in combat in the camp, their fight intense and dangerous. Timothy recognized the fighters as Abbe and Pene-lope.

"Alan!" Adam rushed over, eyes red with worry. "Thank goodness you're here! Stop Chief Master and Penelope before they both get hurt!"

"I'd love to, but..." Timothy was at a loss. Both were superior in martial arts, and their deep-seated enmity made it difficult for him to intervene.

Before he could finish, a silver flash streaked through the air. Penelope's silver spear flew from his hand, spinning several times before embedding itself in the ground.

Penelope's face paled, and as he turned, Abbe's sword pierced through his shoulder.

Penelope's face turned ashen, and he fell to one knee, blood pouring from his shoulder.

Timothy almost rushed forward but managed to hold himself back, watching Abbe intently. Abbe's eyes were bloodshot, his hand shaking uncontrollably as he held the sword.

Penelope looked up, his pale lips curving into a slight smile. "Excellent swordsmanship. I concede."

Abbe's face showed a mix of hatred, humiliation, and something else. He yanked out his sword, gritting his teeth. "Why didn't you fight with all your strength? Do you look down on me, Abbe?"

"Didn't fight with all my strength?" Penelope laughed dryly, clutching his bleeding shoulder. "Facing someone who could kill me at any moment, I'm not that foolish."

Abbe, filled with anger and regret, threw down his sword. "I'll never forgive you, not even in death!"

With that, he turned and ran.

"Abbe!" Without thinking, Timothy chased after him.

Timothy ran out into the busy street but couldn't find any sign of Abbe amid the traffic and crowds. Growing anxious, he asked passersby for information and finally found Abbe sitting in a quiet corner, hugging his knees, shoulders shaking without a sound.

Timothy quietly sat beside him, not saying a word.

They sat in silence, Timothy providing silent companionship.

He thought about how life was full of disappointments and how each person carried their own burdens. Often, people's joys and sorrows didn't align.

Abbe seemed to calm down after a while. He wiped his tears and turned to see Timothy. "Timothy? When did you get here?"

"I've been sitting here for almost an incense stick's time," Timothy replied with a smile, shifting and rubbing his numb behind. "I've been still for so long my butt's gone numb."

"Why didn't you say something earlier?"

"I didn't want to disturb you. I know sometimes you just need to be alone."

After a pause, Abbe asked softly, "Why didn't you stop me earlier?"

"Why would I stop you?" Timothy's tone was matter-of-fact. "You had to vent your anger. If you didn't fight, it would have festered inside you. What if it made you sick? I'd be heartbroken."

"Smooth talker," Abbe muttered, blushing and turning away. "I don't believe you."

Timothy laughed. "Don't believe me? Alright, I'll be honest. It's not that I didn't want to stop you, I didn't dare. With my limited skills, stepping in would have been foolish and suicidal."

"That's nonsense." Abbe glared at him. "I saw you leading the charge yesterday, fearless even in the face of arrows and spears. Are you telling me you're afraid of death? Nonsense!"

Timothy's eyes lit up at the crucial detail in Abbe's words. "Oh! You were hiding somewhere, watching me again, weren't you? Worried I might actually die on the battlefield and not come back?"

He had meant it as a tease, but Abbe's face showed a flash of pain, revealing a deeper truth. Realizing his mistake, Timothy wished he could slap himself for his insensitivity.

"I'm sorry." He pulled Abbe into his arms. "I said something stupid again. I should keep my mouth shut."

Abbe didn't resist, resting quietly in Timothy's embrace. "Lately, I feel like my uncle is watching over me..."

Timothy whispered, "If your uncle could see you now, alive and well, he would be very happy."

Abbe continued, "When I was a child, my father always forced me to study the classics and learn music, chess, calligraphy, and painting. Only my uncle taught me martial arts and swordplay, telling me stories of heroes in troubled times. He said some people's swords are for killing, while others' swords are for saving lives. I asked my uncle, what about my sword? He didn't answer but asked me in return, 'Abbe, what do you want your sword to be?' I shook my head and said I didn't know. My uncle then patted my head and said it was okay, that it was a difficult question and some people never figure it out in their lifetime. He told me I had plenty of time to think about it."

It was the first time Abbe had spoken to Timothy about his childhood. As Timothy listened, he imagined a young Abbe, innocent and pure. His heart softened, and he gently asked, "And did you figure it out later?"

Abbe paused, lowering his eyes in sadness. "All this time, I admired those great heroes with lofty aspirations. I thought wielding my sword was about upholding justice and righteousness. But now, I realize I was wrong. In the end, it was just for myself..."

"There's nothing wrong with that," Timothy said. "Abbe, we're all just ordinary people. No one is born understanding everything, and no one can ensure they never make mistakes. Some things take time to understand, and that's okay. Life is long; we can figure it out together."

"Together?" Abbe was taken aback.

Timothy smiled warmly at him. "Yes, even if it takes a lifetime. I'll be with you."

Timothy's smile was so warm and his eyes so bright, like the scorching sun, that Abbe found it hard to look directly at him.

Adam, who had been waiting for a long time, was overjoyed to see Timothy and Abbe finally returning hand in hand. He rushed over and hugged Abbe tightly. "Chief Master! You're finally back! Adam missed you so much!"

Holding Adam, Abbe felt a flood of memories and couldn't help the tears that welled up again.

Adam and Abbe had much to catch up on, and Timothy, not wanting to disturb them, quietly left alone.

As he approached the King of Nixie's tent, he lifted the flap to see the King of Nixie and Penelope sitting side by side on the bed. Penelope had removed his shirt, exposing a bleeding wound, and the King of Nixie was applying medicine.

The two had been whispering to each other, but stopped immediately upon seeing Timothy. Penelope turned his head away.

The King of Nixie quickly stood up and welcomed Timothy inside with a smile. "Mr. Shaw, you came at the right time. I suddenly have an urgent matter to attend to. You can apply the medicine to Penelope."

Timothy was taken aback, but before he could speak, the King of Nixie patted his shoulder, gave him a knowing wink, and left the tent.

"Wait! Your Highness!" Timothy found himself holding the medicine the King of Nixie had thrust into his hands. With no choice, he approached the bed, seeing Penelope's bare back with a ghastly wound, thinking Abbe's strike had been truly severe.

Nevertheless, it was a self-inflicted wound.

Penelope bit his lip and said in a low voice, "I can apply the medicine myself. You can go."

Timothy thought, "This guy is still so stubborn," and retorted, "Who said I was here to help? I just wanted to see if you were dead or alive. Since you're so lively, I can rest assured."

As Timothy reached out to pat Penelope's shoulder, Penelope turned away, leaving Timothy's hand awkwardly hanging in the air.

Annoyed, Timothy retracted his hand and sneered, "As expected, you, Penelope Morris, always stand tall and never need pity. Fine, you apply the medicine yourself. I want to see how you reach the wound on your back."

Penelope's face showed unbearable humiliation. Seeing Timothy actually throw the medicine bottle in front of him made his face turn even paler.

Without a word, he grabbed the bottle, poured the powder into his palm, and tried to reach his back, but he couldn't reach the wound. Even when he barely managed to touch it, the medicine spilled everywhere, littering the bed and floor.

Penelope was mortified but remained silent, stubbornly trying again, his trembling hand making it even harder.

From start to finish, Timothy stood aside with his arms crossed, watching coldly.

When Penelope failed for the third time, knocking the medicine bottle to the ground, Timothy finally couldn't stand it anymore. He walked over, picked up the bottle, and found it empty.

Scoffing, Timothy left the tent.

As he walked out, he heard a loud crash behind him, knowing it was Penelope throwing a tantrum. Ignoring him, Timothy returned to his own tent.

Rummaging through his belongings, Timothy found a few more bottles of medicine and went back to the King of Nixie's tent. Inside, he saw Penelope lying on the bed, his long hair tangled and sticking to his bloody wound, a disturbing sight.

Timothy approached, ready to help, but Penelope shuddered and pushed him away.

"Why did you come back? Can't you just let me die? Or do you want to see me suffer? Are you satisfied now?"

Timothy felt a surge of anger. "Do you have any sense? I'm trying to help, and this is the thanks I get? Do I owe you something?"

Penelope laughed bitterly. "Help? What good intentions could you have?"

Timothy, exasperated by Penelope's stubbornness but unable to leave him untreated, threatened, "Keep talking like that, and I'll be rough with you!"

Penelope's eyes reddened as he glared at Timothy. "You wouldn't dare!"

"Watch me!" Timothy grabbed Penelope's hand and pushed him to the ground. Shocked by the sudden aggression, Penelope struggled, shouting, "Let me go!"

Ignoring his protests, Timothy straddled him, pinning his arms behind his back with one hand and grabbing a bottle of medicine with the other. Using his teeth to pull off the cork, he poured the powder onto Penelope's wound.

Penelope screamed in pain, writhing under Timothy, his body trembling. "Timothy! You're doing this on purpose!"

"You brought this on yourself!"

Timothy rubbed the powder into Penelope's wound. Penelope's constant struggling made it difficult, but Timothy managed. Then he flipped Penelope over and repeated the process on his chest wound, pouring the entire bottle onto it.

Penelope was paralyzed by the pain, sweat beading on his forehead, his lower lip almost bitten through.

"Finally feeling it?" Timothy, out of breath from the effort, sneered, "Let's see if you still want to talk back!"

Despite the pain, Penelope remained silent, tears rolling down his cheeks. Turning his face away, he couldn't stop the tears from falling.

Cursing under his breath, Timothy grabbed a cloth, pressing it to Penelope's wound, and wrapped it around him.

Penelope, having given up resistance, allowed Timothy to bind his wound. Timothy's movements became gentler as he realized Penelope had stopped fighting.

To bandage the wound, Timothy had to lean close, their faces almost touching, noses nearly brushing. Penelope's bare chest and tear-streaked face made it look like Timothy was doing something improper.

Penelope's chest heaved, his breath ragged, a faint blush coloring his pale face.

Finally finished, Timothy looked like he had fought a battle himself, his hands covered in Penelope's blood.

"What are you doing?"

A voice from behind made Timothy turn. The King of Nixie stood in the doorway, staring at the disheveled pair and the mess.

"I'm done," Timothy said, wiping sweat from his brow.

"Done with what?" The King of Nixie looked from Timothy to Penelope, confused. "Done with what?"

"Applying the medicine, of course," Timothy replied innocently.

The King of Nixie stared at the scene, bewildered by the sight that resembled a crime scene.

Chapter Forty-Eight: Substitute the Plum for the Peach

Time was of the essence, and the situation in Poiema grew tenser by the day. However, once they marched north to Poiema, Gaylord would become their rear. If Gaylord fell, the King of Nixie's army would be attacked from both front and rear, making it imperative to leave someone behind to guard it.

After much consideration, Timothy decided that Penelope was the best candidate. This was not only because Penelope, as a local leader, had considerable experience in city defense but also to keep him and Abbe apart, preventing further conflict between the two sworn enemies.

Penelope did not object. In fact, since that day when Timothy had treated his wounds with brute force, Penelope seemed to have temporarily become more compliant, no longer constantly opposing Timothy. Whenever their eyes met, he quickly looked away, and his sarcastic remarks had significantly decreased.

While Penelope had become "compliant," it was now Timothy who felt uneasy. From the beginning, he had been deceived by Penelope's compliance, leading to his downfall. As a result, Timothy always associated a compliant Penelope with a belly full of schemes.

It was hard to tell whether he was once bitten, twice shy, or if he had developed a tendency for self-abuse.

In any case, once everything was arranged, Timothy followed the King of Nixie's army out of the city, leading the newly recruited Gaylord soldiers—a total of eighty thousand troops—marching grandly towards Poiema.

Just after Penelope had seen off the King of Nixie, Timothy, and the others from Gaylord, he received a report from his subordinates saying that two men claiming to be old acquaintances of Timothy from Poiema had arrived and requested to see him. Without much thought, Penelope ordered his men to bring the two to the hall.

Soon, two men were led into the hall. Penelope scrutinized them closely. One had a commanding presence with sharp eyebrows and bright eyes, while the other had a baby face, handsome and lively. The baby-faced one introduced himself as Kalle, and the other as Arya.

"Timothy has already led the troops out of the city," Penelope said calmly. "You are too late."

"What?!" Arya exclaimed, "How long has he been gone?"

"He left early yesterday morning."

Arya lowered his head in thought, then said, "I will go after him." Kalle quickly grabbed Arya's sleeve, saying, "Absolutely not! They are going to war; it's too dangerous. You cannot risk yourself!"

Penelope silently observed them and then interjected, "Who exactly are you to Timothy? Why are you looking for him?"

Arya and Kalle exchanged a glance. Finally, Kalle hesitantly spoke, "We... are distant relatives of Timothy, looking to seek refuge with him."

"Distant relatives?" Penelope mused, looking thoughtful. "In that case, stay here in Gaylord and wait for Timothy to return victorious."

Without giving them a chance to argue, Penelope ordered his men to escort Arya and Kalle out and arrange for them to stay in a guest room by the study.

That night, Penelope worked late into the night, finally finishing his tasks around midnight. Rubbing his temples, he donned a robe and called for his steward to ask if the two guests had settled in. The steward replied that they were staying in a side room near the study. Penelope nodded, deciding to visit these supposed relatives of Timothy personally.

As he walked towards the study, he suddenly saw a figure hastily crossing the courtyard. Startled, Penelope retreated into the shadows to observe.

The figure was cloaked in black, face obscured, moving quickly and looking around nervously. Growing suspicious, Penelope quietly followed.

The cloaked figure went straight to the stables and started leading a horse out.

"Stop!" Penelope emerged from the darkness, blocking the figure's path.

Startled, the figure turned to run, but Penelope was quicker. He lunged forward, pulling off the cloak.

"You...?" Penelope gasped, recognizing the face beneath the cloak.

It was Arya, who had claimed to be Timothy's distant relative.

Arya said nothing, grabbing the reins and trying to mount the horse. But Penelope wasn't about to let him escape. He quickly seized Arya's wrist, and to his surprise, Arya offered little resistance, lacking any martial skills. Within moments, Penelope had him pinned to the ground, hands tied behind his back.

"Who are you? What are you up to?" Penelope demanded, his eyes sharp as knives.

"Are you Penelope?" Arya asked, struggling beneath him.

Penelope replied coldly, "So what if I am?"

Arya continued, "Your family has been loyal to the Harris family for generations, right?"

Penelope's face darkened. "What are you getting at?"

Arya, panting, said, "Then you should step back! Do you know the punishment for defying your sovereign?"

"Defying the sovereign...?" Penelope was stunned. A sudden realization struck him, and he quickly released Arya. "You... you're..."

Arya finally got up, shakily, and gasped, "Bring me a bucket of water."

In the moonlight, Penelope could hardly believe his eyes. The man claiming to be Arya washed away the makeup on his face, revealing his true identity—it was none other than the Emperor of Great Alvah, Christopher.

It turned out that the woman Arya had brought before Christopher in Temple Lrisa was a master of disguise. Her skills were so extraordinary that she had swapped the appearances of Christopher and Arya flawlessly. Even though Christopher had been mentally prepared, seeing his doppelgänger was still a shock.

"I can't believe such remarkable disguise skills exist. If I hadn't seen it with my own eyes, I wouldn't have believed it," Penelope said.

"Neither did I. Even now, it feels surreal. But thanks to this disguise, I escaped from the heavily guarded palace, from the prison that held me for over twenty years," Christopher replied.

"So the one currently confined in the palace is Arya, your bodyguard, correct?"

"Yes."

"But there's one thing I don't understand," Penelope said, frowning. "No matter how perfect the disguise, it can only deceive for a while. The false can never become true. Over time, the ruse will be uncovered. Why did Your Majesty take such a great risk to leave the palace?"

Christopher lowered his eyes, speaking softly, "I had a constant feeling of unease, as if something big was about to happen. Disguising and leaving the palace was Arya's suggestion. Initially, I was uncertain, but the thought of possibly seeing Timothy made me disregard everything else."

Penelope's eyes widened. "Your Majesty took such a risk just to see Timothy?"

Christopher smiled bitterly. "That was my personal desire. After escaping, Kalle and I soon heard about Timothy and the King of Nixie's uprising in Gaylord. We also heard that Bowie was rallying the states and counties to suppress them. I was relieved that I heeded Arya's advice to escape. If I had been captured by Bowie and used as a puppet, it would have been disastrous for Timothy and his allies."

"So Your Majesty wants to catch up to Timothy to legitimize their cause?"

"Exactly."

"But Your Majesty, I still believe this is unwise," Penelope said earnestly. "The battlefield is dangerous. You cannot risk yourself. Moreover, even if you don't go to the front lines, as long as you stay in Gaylord and declare Bowie and his followers as traitors, you will already be raising the banner of justice for us. Your presence in Gaylord will reassure the soldiers attacking Poiema, allowing Timothy to focus on the battle without worries."

Christopher lowered his eyes, pondering for a long time.

"Indeed, you have a point. That is the safest course of action. However..." Christopher's tone shifted, and he looked Penelope in the eye. "I still feel I should be with Timothy."

Penelope, moved by Christopher's gaze, asked, "Why?"

Christopher gazed into the distance, his eyes gentle yet unwaveringly resolute. "Because I can no longer endure it. I don't want to hide under the protection of others any longer. Perhaps my strength is still insufficient to protect those I love. But those soldiers who fight and bleed for me, for Great Alvah—aren't they all my people? How can I cower in a safe corner while they charge into battle? I can't do it. I will not let the soldiers down!"

Hearing Christopher's impassioned words, Penelope found himself looking at the ruler of Great Alvah with newfound respect.

Back in Sunder, Penelope had heard bits and pieces about Christopher from the King of Nixie. Among the emperor's sons, Christopher was not the most favored. He rose to power largely due to Queen Owen.

It was not that Christopher had sought Queen Owen's assistance; rather, she had secretly eliminated all his rivals. From the moment she married Christopher, Queen Owen had begun plotting her power grab. She placed her pieces strategically, putting Christopher on the throne as a stepping stone in her quest for control.

When this unsuspecting young prince ascended to the throne, he found himself surrounded by Queen Owen's people. When she presented herself as a benefactor, how could Christopher refuse her? How could he not surrender his power?

Yet now, it seemed Christopher was not entirely without backbone. He had finally reached his breaking point.

It wasn't just the battlefield—no matter what dangers lay ahead, Christopher would face them head-on.

Realizing this, Penelope abandoned any thoughts of persuading Christopher to stay in Gaylord. He stepped forward and knelt on one knee before him.

"Your Majesty, it is Great Alvah's fortune to have an emperor who cares so deeply for his people. Penelope is willing to serve you loyally, unto death!"

The next morning, Penelope dispatched two highly skilled martial arts guards to escort Christopher out of the city.

Christopher did not inform Kalle of his plans to pursue Timothy. He didn't want to worry or endanger Kalle, who had already been exhausted from protecting Christopher during their escape from the palace. Since Kalle didn't know martial arts and couldn't fight, Christopher hoped he could stay safely in Gaylord and wait for their triumphant return.

Once outside Gaylord, Christopher and his guards rode tirelessly for a day and a night. They finally reached the outskirts of Poiema, where they found not a living army but a battlefield strewn with corpses.

It seemed a fierce battle had recently taken place. Christopher grew more anxious, fearing that the King of Nixie's forces had been ambushed or surrounded. Although the various forces of Great Alvah had yet to mobilize against them, Bowie and Queen Owen's factions had already gathered troops near Poiema in response to the court's call. If the King of Nixie's army did not swiftly capture Poiema, the prolonged conflict would increasingly disadvantage Timothy and the King of Nixie.

Christopher pressed on until he reached the outskirts of Poiema, where he heard the deafening sounds of battle. The King of Nixie's banners flew high in the main camp, while arrows rained down from the city walls and siege engines hurled stones. The fighting was intense.

Knowing Timothy was in the midst of this chaos, Christopher could no longer hold back. He spurred his horse forward, but his guards quickly restrained him. "Your Majesty, it's too dangerous to enter the fray!"

Christopher's expression was resolute. "I've come this far; I cannot retreat now. I know what I must do. Do not try to stop me."

With that, he lashed his horse forward, leaving his guards behind as he charged toward the King of Nixie's main camp.

As Christopher, alone on horseback, burst into the King of Nixie's ranks, the soldiers were disheartened by the stalemate.

Poiema's walls were higher and stronger than Gaylord's, and the resistance was fiercer.

Suddenly, the drums of the King of Nixie's army thundered like a storm.

Everyone turned to see a man in a black cloak standing on the drum platform, wielding the drumsticks with fervor. Beside him, a banner depicting a majestic white tiger fluttered in the wind.

"It's the White Tiger Banner!"

An excited cry rose from the ranks.

In Great Alvah, two banners symbolized supreme authority, and the White Tiger Banner was one of them. The white tiger, a beast of valor and conquest, symbolized invincibility. Thus, this banner was the emblem of the emperor's command in war. Its presence signified the bearer wielded supreme authority.

The appearance of the White Tiger Banner among the King of Nixie's forces instantly revitalized the soldiers, filling them with renewed vigor and morale.

Conversely, the sight of the banner, which should have been in the palace, now among their enemies, threw the defenders of Poiema into disarray and panic.

Timothy, amidst the chaos, noticed this and was stunned. He watched the figure beating the drum, feeling a pang of familiarity.

"Christopher?!"

The name flashed through Timothy's mind like a lightning bolt. His heart pounded in his chest. He couldn't believe his eyes. Christopher was supposed to be confined in the palace by Bowie and Queen Owen. Why was he here, with the White Tiger Banner?

Without further thought, Timothy galloped to the drum platform.

"Your Majesty!" Timothy leaped onto the platform, shouting.

Christopher's hands froze, and the drumsticks fell to the ground. He turned slowly.

Timothy, clad in battle armor, his face hardened by war, exuded a heroic aura.

Christopher, his face as delicate as ever, now bore a look of resilience and determination.

"What are you doing here?!"

Timothy's face flushed with urgency, disregarding protocol. He grabbed Christopher's shoulders, shielding him with his body. "This is a battlefield! Do you realize how dangerous this is?"

Christopher, feeling Timothy's embrace for the first time in ages, felt tears welling up. Gazing into Timothy's eyes, he said, "I wanted to see you. I couldn't wait any longer."

Timothy felt a pang of sorrow, holding Christopher tightly. "I'm sorry, Your Majesty. I came too late."

"Will you blame me?" Christopher asked, his heart pounding.

"No, seeing you here makes me happier than words can express!" Timothy squeezed Christopher's hand. "I have much to say, but now, amidst this battle, I cannot let personal feelings hinder our cause."

He was about to turn away when Christopher grabbed his hand. "I will fight with you!" Christopher's eyes blazed with determination. "I want to stand by your side."

Chapter Forty-Nine: Karmic Retribution

The deafening drums reverberated across the sky. The moment Christopher appeared with the White Tiger Banner among the King of Nixie's troops, the tide of battle turned dramatically. Under the ferocious and relentless assaults of the King of Nixie's army, the gates of Poiema finally collapsed with a thunderous crash.

The army surged into the city like a tide, splitting into three divisions to launch a full-scale assault on the imperial palace.

"Your Majesty, quickly, mount the horse!" Timothy rode up to Christopher, extending his hand. Christopher gladly took Timothy's hand, and in that instant, he was struck by how much had changed. Timothy's hands, now calloused and rough, were a testament to his hard-earned growth, yet they retained the same warmth.

Without much thought, Christopher was pulled up onto the saddle, sitting behind Timothy.

Timothy turned back, teasing him with a smile, "Your Majesty, you're so light! Have you been eating properly?"

Christopher pressed his face against Timothy's back, murmuring, "It's because I've missed you..."

Timothy chuckled, "Then you should hold on tight, Your Majesty, so the wind doesn't blow you away."

Christopher quickly wrapped his arms around Timothy's waist, and with a flick of the reins, they galloped toward the imperial palace.

Despite the chaos around them, Christopher felt an unprecedented sense of security, holding Timothy close.

He recalled the first time he met Timothy in Hall Zona, back when Timothy was just a roguish street rat with a bit of charm but plenty of insolence and mischief.

Now, after three months apart, Timothy had changed and grown.

"Timothy, who taught you archery?" Christopher asked, amazed by Timothy's swift and accurate shots.

"My master did!"

"Who is your master?"

"His name is Abbe." At the mention of Abbe, a gentle smile played on Timothy's lips.

Christopher couldn't see Timothy's expression, but holding him tight, he felt a mix of emotions.

In the days they were apart, Timothy had met many people and experienced many things, which had changed him. He had become more composed, more manly, and a more formidable warrior.

In contrast, Christopher's difficult step forward might seem like standing still to Timothy. This realization filled Christopher with both frustration and determination. It felt as if Timothy had grown wings, soaring higher and farther from his reach.

Christopher was the emperor, destined to rule the land.

"Your Majesty!" A familiar voice snapped Christopher out of his thoughts. He looked up to see the King of Nixie riding towards them, bowing in salute. "Your Majesty! Forgive me for being late to your rescue!"

"Imperial Uncle, rise," Christopher said. "In these urgent times, there is no need for formalities."

The King of Nixie looked at Christopher with undisguised affection in his eyes.

"Report! The Black Tortoise Gate has been breached!" A messenger rode up to report.

"And Queen Owen and Bowie?" the King of Nixie asked.

"Queen Owen is in the inner court, currently under guard. Bowie's whereabouts are unknown."

"Unknown?" The King of Nixie frowned. "Did he sense something and flee?"

"Leaving Queen Owen behind? Escaping alone?" Timothy found it hard to believe. "Aren't they in this together? He wouldn't just abandon her without a word."

"Perhaps Queen Owen couldn't leave," Christopher speculated.

"Why do you say that?" Timothy asked.

"Queen Owen is pregnant, making her movement difficult. Moreover, her power and wealth come from controlling me as her puppet. Without me and without her status as queen, she truly has nothing," Christopher explained, his tone calm but laden with bitterness and helplessness. Timothy and the King of Nixie exchanged heavy glances, unable to find words.

"Your Majesty, those days are over," Timothy finally said. "From today onward, you won't have to endure such humiliation."

Christopher, silent for a moment, then lifted his head, staring at the smoke-covered palace. "Yes, today, it all ends."

As Timothy and his men entered the palace through the Black Tortoise Gate, the imperial guards continued their desperate resistance. But when Christopher ascended to the Hall Bluma, the symbol of ultimate authority in Great Alvah, and when Timothy brandished the Banner, a symbol of ceasefire and peace, both sides dropped their weapons in unison.

Amidst the lingering smoke, the palace lay in ruin. Bodies were strewn everywhere, and blood splattered the steps and pillars. To Christopher, who had grown accustomed to this palace, everything now seemed strange and foreign.

Half a year ago, before meeting Timothy, Christopher might have only dreamed of such a scene. He never imagined witnessing it in his lifetime.

But the day had finally come.

Christopher stood tall and proud before the majestic Hall Bluma, trying to calm his excitement. The wind, laden with the scent of blood, blew past him as he gazed down at the thousands of soldiers kneeling before him. Among them were both the King of Nixie's troops and the imperial guards. Moments ago, they had been mortal enemies, but now they were united, bowing in reverence and chanting in unison.

This absolute power, the very thing Queen Owen and Bowie had committed treason for, now lay in Christopher's hands. The feeling was intoxicating, making him understand why they had been driven to madness by it. For the first time since ascending the throne, Christopher felt he truly wielded power.

"Timothy," he called out, taking a deep breath.

"Your servant is here," Timothy replied, rising. In front of the assembled officials and soldiers, he dared not be informal, his face showing deep respect for his sovereign.

"You reclaimed this kingdom for me," Christopher said, gazing at him. "How should I thank you?"

"I did nothing special," Timothy quickly responded. "It was mainly the King of Nixie and the others..."

Before he could finish, Christopher leaned in and planted a kiss on his lips.

Timothy was stunned.

In front of the entire army!

Timothy glanced around in panic, relieved to see everyone kneeling and seemingly unaware of their actions.

"That's my reward," Christopher said with a mischievous smile. "And you can't refuse it."

"Your Majesty..." Timothy sighed, then quickly pecked Christopher's lips again when he was sure no one was watching.

"Dig up the entire Poiema if you have to, but find Bowie!" the King of Nixie commanded, and hundreds of search teams spread out.

By nightfall, the battles had ceased, and Poiema's gates were shut, with only the east gate, Syed, remaining open. A curfew was imposed, and the streets were empty except for the patrols.

This did not include Abbe.

Leaping across rooftops, Abbe moved swiftly and silently until he reached a mansion. He waited until a figure emerged, sneaking out cautiously.

"Bowie," Abbe called quietly. The man froze, turning to see a familiar silhouette under the moonlight.

"You've got the wrong person! I'm not Bowie!" the man denied.

Abbe smirked, leaping down and approaching. The man, seeing Abbe's face, turned pale with fright.

"Payton!?" The man's legs gave out, and he collapsed onto the ground, fear-stricken. "Aren't you supposed to be dead? Are you a ghost?"

Since the King of Nixie's army had breached Poiema, Abbe had taken advantage of the chaos to infiltrate the city. While Timothy and the others attacked the palace, he had been scouring Poiema for Bowie's whereabouts. Upon learning that the King of Nixie's forces were about to capture the city, Bowie had fled the palace, hiding in his home's filthy latrine for hours to avoid detection. He only dared to sneak out under the cover of darkness, but he walked right into Abbe's ambush.

Abbe didn't bother correcting Bowie's mistaken belief. He advanced slowly, his voice icy. "Why are you so afraid of me?"

"Don't come near me! It's not my fault!" Bowie was pale as a sheet, his voice trembling with desperation. "It was the Queen! She ordered the massacre of your family, not me!"

With a swift motion, Abbe drew his sword, giving Bowie no time to explain. He charged, and Bowie, scrambling to escape, was swiftly struck down. Abbe's sword pierced Bowie's thigh, and he fell, screaming in agony.

Abbe's eyes burned with fury, hatred, and sorrow as he glared at the man writhing on the ground. Without hesitation, he raised his sword, aiming for Bowie's heart.

"Stop!" Just then, someone grabbed Abbe's wrist.

Abbe paused, looking up to see Timothy. He tried to break free, but Timothy held firm. They stood locked in a struggle, the sword suspended in mid-air.

"Let go!" Abbe demanded.

"No!" Timothy tightened his grip. "I don't want this scum's blood on your hands!"

As Abbe struggled, footsteps approached. The King of Nixie entered the courtyard with his guards. They quickly subdued Bowie.

"Mr. Simpson, stay calm," the King of Nixie said, stepping forward. "Bowie's crimes are heinous. Killing him with one stroke is too merciful."

"He murdered my father and exterminated my family! If I don't kill him myself, what meaning is there in my life?" Abbe's voice shook with rage.

"Mr. Simpson," the King of Nixie replied calmly, "don't you want to know how your father was killed? Tomorrow, His Majesty will hold a public trial at the White Horse Temple."

"A public trial?" Abbe echoed, taken aback.

"Yes," the King of Nixie confirmed. "Queen Owen and Bowie's crimes will be laid bare for all of Poiema to see."

Abbe looked down, his expression conflicted.

"Abbe," Timothy whispered, wiping the blood from Abbe's sword, "let the law take its course. This villain will face justice."

Abbe looked at Timothy, then at the restrained Bowie. After a long, tense silence, he finally lowered his sword.

The next day, the White Horse Temple in Poiema was packed. On a high platform before the Grand Hall, Bowie knelt, disheveled and dressed in prison garb. Queen Owen should have been beside him, but her advanced pregnancy prevented her from being brought to the scene.

Opposite the platform sat Christopher, dressed in a black dragon-embroidered robe, exuding a silent but formidable authority.

"The criminal Bowie, as an imperial relative, harbored treacherous intentions, colluding with Queen Owen to manipulate the emperor and officials, engaging in factional strife, and framing loyal ministers like Pei Yuan and Payton..." The National Court official loudly recited the charges. The list was long, detailing Bowie's and Queen Owen's crimes, including corruption, bribery, and forging imperial decrees.

Throughout the reading, Bowie remained silent, his face ashen. The crowd below murmured, reacting to the revelations.

"Justice is served! Bowie deserved this! It's karma!"

"Too bad it came too late. If it had come sooner, Mr. Simpson wouldn't have died in vain."

"Indeed, Mr. Simpson was a rare honest and upright official, loved by the people. It's tragic he met such an end."

Timothy, Abbe, and Adam stood amidst the crowd, hearing every word. Adam was appalled by the charges. "With crimes like that, Bowie should be executed by lingchi!"

Timothy, however, focused on Abbe. Since the trial began, Abbe had been silent, his eyes fixed on the platform, his face clouded with grief.

As the charges were read, Abbe finally turned away.

"Abbe, aren't you going to stay?" Timothy asked.

Abbe shook his head. "There's no need. Everything is clear now."

"Where are you going?"

"Don't worry," Abbe said, not looking back. "I won't leave without a word. I just need some time alone."

With that, Abbe pushed through the crowd and left.

Abbe wandered aimlessly, eventually buying a jug of wine and some incense. He walked east, exiting through Syed Gate.

Beyond the gate lay a graveyard, desolate and sparsely populated. Abbe walked silently among the tombstones, the only sounds coming from the wind and the occasional owl's mournful cry.

Unknown to Abbe, Timothy and Adam had followed him. They kept their distance, watching as Abbe stopped at a grave. He knelt, brushed the dust from the tombstone, and revealed the name "Payton."

"Is Chief Master paying respects?" Adam whispered, craning his neck. "Whose grave is that?"

"Too far to see," Timothy replied thoughtfully. "But it's likely related to the Simpson family."

"Could it be Mr. Simpson?" Adam gasped.

"Shh," Timothy hushed him.

Abbe lit the incense, placing it before the grave. He poured some wine as an offering, then stood in silent contemplation.

Timothy's intuition was correct. This was the Simpson family burial site, and the grave bore the name "Payton."

Payton had been a beloved official, respected by the people. When the Simpson family was executed, many came to pay their last respects. After their execution, compassionate citizens had gathered the bodies and buried them here, outside Poiema.

This was something Timothy had learned only recently.

At this moment, Timothy did not know all the details. He only saw that Abbe, despite having avenged his family and cleared the Simpson family's name, looked burdened and lost. Instead of joy and satisfaction, there was a haunted, distant look in his eyes.

"Alan, aren't you going to comfort Chief Master?" Adam couldn't bear it any longer. He looked up at Timothy, his face filled with concern. "Besides his uncle, you're the person Chief Master trusts the most."

"He trusts me... the most?" Timothy was taken aback.

"Yes." Adam nodded confidently. "I don't know where Chief Master went or what he did, but if he didn't trust you, he wouldn't have come back. I've been by his side these past days, and it's clear to me. Even though he doesn't say it, he's already let go of his doubts and suspicions about you."

Timothy managed a bitter smile. He wanted to be there for Abbe, to give him a hug or at least hold his hand, offering some warmth. He had done the same in Gaylord.

But was that really enough?

"Abbe doesn't need comfort right now," Timothy said softly.

Adam's eyes widened. "Not comfort? Then what?"

Timothy looked at Abbe's retreating figure, falling into a deep silence.

On the surface, Abbe seemed to have returned to normal, even offering Timothy advice and support. However, no matter how much he pretended to have moved on, the shadows of sorrow remained etched in his features, refusing to be dispelled.

The knot buried deep in Abbe's heart was not something that could be untangled with a few words or in a short time. Frankly, Timothy felt helpless and at a loss. But he wouldn't give up. Even if it took longer, he would keep searching until he found the key to unlock Abbe's heart.

Abbe wandered aimlessly through the desolate graveyard, his steps slow and unsteady. He reached a particular grave, knelt down, and gently brushed away the thick layer of dust on the tombstone. The name "Payton" emerged, faint but legible.

Abbe placed the incense in front of the grave, lit it, and poured some wine as an offering. Then he stood motionless, staring at the tombstone, lost in thought.

"Is Chief Master here to pay respects?" Adam whispered, straining to see. "Whose grave is that?"

"It's too far to see clearly," Timothy replied thoughtfully. "But it's likely someone from the Simpson family."

"Could it be Mr. Simpson?" Adam guessed, eyes wide.

"Shh," Timothy hushed him, pressing a finger to his lips.

Abbe stood alone before the grave, lost in memories. This was the resting place of his family, and the name "Payton" was etched into the stone. Payton had been a beloved official, respected by the people. When the Simpson family was executed, many had come to pay their last respects. Compassionate citizens had gathered the bodies and buried them here, outside Poiema.

Timothy and Adam watched from a distance, aware that Abbe needed this moment alone.

Abbe's heart was heavy with grief and unresolved pain. He had avenged his family, but the emptiness and sorrow remained. Timothy knew that the path to healing would be long and arduous, but he was determined to walk it with Abbe, every step of the way.

Back at the White Horse Temple, the public trial continued. Bowie knelt in his prison garb, his crimes laid bare for all to see. The people murmured, reacting to the revelations of his misdeeds.

Justice was finally being served, and Bowie would face the consequences of his actions. But for Abbe, the true challenge lay in finding peace within himself. Timothy resolved to be there for him, no matter how long it took.

The sky darkened as evening approached, casting long shadows over the graveyard. Abbe remained by the grave, lost in thought, while Timothy and Adam watched from afar, ready to support him whenever he needed it.

Extra Story: Beauty Mark

In the searing heat of July, Poiema transitioned from the late summer to the early autumn of golden cassia flowers.

A devastating war had upheaved the Great Alvah court's power structure. However, the smoke of battle would eventually dissipate with time. For the ordinary citizens of Poiema, the struggles for power above them were always irrelevant. The war brought them nothing more than a day's worth of the clamor of arms and armor, serving only as a topic for idle chatter over meals.

However, the situation was entirely different for Christopher, the ruler of Great Alvah.

At this very moment in Hall Zona, an unimaginable scene was unfolding—one that Christopher would never have believed possible a month ago. He, Christopher, the ruler of Great Alvah, was seated in Hall Zona, quietly listening to a minister standing before him, reporting on state affairs.

Despite his status as a monarch, Christopher had been completely ignorant of state matters since his ascension to the throne. All affairs, whether military or civil, were tightly controlled by Queen Owen. Christopher knew nothing and dared not inquire. Now, the situation had changed, and Christopher had finally seized control. The minister before him, named Nicholas Wilkinson, had been speaking non-stop for the past half-hour. Christopher did not interrupt, keeping his head down as he perused the memorials in his hands, his expression somewhat distracted, his posture rigid, and his fair face faintly flushed.

Christopher's distraction was not due to fatigue or boredom but because of an unspeakable discomfort. Any slight movement caused the large plug in his rear to grind mercilessly against his sensitive spot. How could he maintain composure if he accidentally lost control in front of his ministers?

The culprit responsible for this predicament stood obediently beside him.

Christopher glanced sideways at Timothy, meeting his deeply meaningful gaze. Christopher's heart trembled, and he quickly looked away.

Earlier, Timothy and Christopher were indulging in their usual passion in Hall Zona. Just as they were in the throes of their love-making, an eunuch announced Chancellor Nicholas's arrival. Christopher wanted to dismiss him, but Timothy persuaded him otherwise. According to Timothy, Christopher needed to establish himself as a wise and receptive ruler among his ministers, especially after just taking power. He couldn't afford to neglect his duties for personal reasons.

Christopher saw the logic in Timothy's words, but Timothy had just finished inside him. If he got up now, the semen would surely leak out. In a flurry, he used the plug to seal his rear, then straightened his clothes and opened the door to receive Nicholas as if nothing had happened.

Nicholas was an intriguing figure. Though from a prestigious family, he differed from those disdainful of the court. He was a passionate young man dedicated to governance, having served as a secretary under Payton.

Unfortunately, his rigid and unyielding nature made it impossible for him to tolerate the corruption of Bowie, leading him to resign in frustration. Only now was he reinstated as Chancellor.

Nicholas's flaw was his inability to stop talking once he started, oblivious to Christopher's distraction as he continued his fervent speech.

"Since the fall, the barbarians have repeatedly invaded our borders, plundering and killing, causing immense suffering. The court should strengthen border defenses and send reinforcements to repel the invaders. However, with Bowie and his ilk in control, the treasury is severely depleted, leaving us with inadequate military funds. Therefore, fiscal reform is imperative. I implore Your Majesty to implement the new policies I've proposed, eliminate outdated practices, strengthen our military, and protect our people."

Nicholas concluded his lengthy speech, but Christopher, feeling awkward and unsure of how to respond, turned to Timothy.

"What do you think, Timothy?" Christopher asked, signaling Timothy with a glance.

Timothy, understanding Christopher's plight, cleared his throat. "Mr. Wilkinson's concern for the state is commendable. However, I must say, his proposed reforms seem...excessive."

"Mr. Wilkinson, your policies are thorough, but aren't you afraid that such drastic changes might cause problems?" Timothy said.

"You...you insolent fool!" Nicholas, unaccustomed to such coarse language, turned red and white with anger. "Reforms must be decisive! Hesitation will only hinder progress! My policies are not impulsive. When I served as county magistrate, my reforms were well-received by the people. You know nothing!"

"Mr. Wilkinson's words are..." Christopher tried to intervene but felt a sudden pang of pleasure from the plug, making him moan involuntarily.

Shocked, he quickly covered his mouth.

Timothy and Nicholas turned their attention to Christopher, whose face was now crimson.

"Your Majesty, are you unwell?" Nicholas asked, stepping forward.

Timothy quickly wrapped an arm around Christopher, supporting him.

"His Majesty has been overworking himself," Timothy said. "I've advised him to delegate more to capable ministers like Mr.

Wilkinson. Your Majesty, let Mr. Wilkinson handle more of these matters."

Nicholas, unable to argue, had no choice but to bow and leave.

"He's quite a character," Timothy remarked, picking up Nicholas's memorial. He had a close relationship with Christopher and didn't stand on ceremony. "His writing is impressive, though."

Christopher, his arms wrapped around Timothy, whispered, "People are gone, so why pretend?"

Timothy smiled, holding Christopher's hand.

"He's talented, but reforms must be gradual," Timothy said. "Nicholas is a valuable asset, but we must be cautious."

Christopher nodded, his body relaxing in Timothy's embrace.

Christopher teased for a long time, but seeing that Timothy remained unmoved, he pushed Timothy into a nearby chair. Before Timothy could react, Christopher straddled his lap, spreading his legs intimately.

"You may be nice to him, but he doesn't necessarily think highly of you," Christopher said, then lowered his head, biting and teasing Timothy's earlobe with his tongue. "Didn't you see how he looked at you just now? As if he wanted to flay you alive."

Timothy laughed, "If he can devise a practical reform, I wouldn't mind being flayed alive by him."

"That won't do," Christopher released Timothy's ear, cupping Timothy's face and speaking firmly, "You are mine, and no one can lay a finger on you."

With that, their lips met in a passionate kiss.

Perhaps it was just an illusion, but Timothy found that Christopher seemed increasingly clingy recently.

This wasn't to say they were always inseparable. On the contrary, because Timothy refused any official position and the court was in a state of rebuilding, many matters required Christopher's personal attention. Even after the war, their meetings weren't much more frequent than before.

Thus, whenever they did meet, Christopher would cling to Timothy as if his life depended on it, unwilling to let him go until they had their fill of intimacy.

In truth, Christopher was still afraid of being lonely.

Timothy understood this to some extent. Christopher had long been isolated, with no consorts or children to keep him company. The vast palace was his to guard alone. In the past, such loneliness, though hard, became bearable with time.

But now things were different; fate had brought Timothy into Christopher's life.

Timothy filled the void of loneliness, allowing Christopher to experience genuine affection for the first time. Once one tastes sweetness, it becomes harder to endure loneliness.

In their past intimacies, Christopher had always been passive.

But now, Christopher was becoming increasingly proactive, passionately engaging Timothy, forcing his almost waning desire to rise again, pressing hard against Christopher's waist.

Timothy placed the memorials on the table and embraced Christopher's slender waist, his hand moving to the toy inside Christopher, slowly teasing it.

Christopher shivered, moaning softly, "Enough, stop that."

"Didn't you put this toy in yourself?" Timothy asked.

"I don't want this toy," Christopher replied.

"Oh? What do you want then?" Timothy teased.

Christopher bit his lip in frustration, leaning in to bite Timothy's lip hard, "You know exactly what I want."

Timothy gasped, touching the bitten lip and seeing blood on his fingers.

That drop of blood ignited Timothy's primal desire.

He swiftly pulled out the toy, tossing the lubricant-soaked item aside, and without allowing the flesh to close, he thrust his rigid member deep into Christopher.

As the thick shaft pierced him, Christopher cried out in pleasure, his body trembling and clutching Timothy's neck tightly.

With his long-awaited craving finally filled, Christopher moaned unabashedly, writhing on Timothy's lap, eagerly moving his hips to meet Timothy's thrusts, his voice growing louder and more wanton with each movement.

Christopher's licentious display only fueled Timothy's dominant urges. He tore open Christopher's clothes, roughly kneading his swollen nipples. Every squeeze made Christopher gasp, his inner walls contracting involuntarily.

Unable to resist the intoxicating sensation, Timothy grabbed Christopher's buttocks, thrusting vigorously.

"Timothy... stay with me, don't go..." Christopher pleaded between gasps.

Timothy didn't respond, his thrusts growing deeper and harder, making Christopher cry out and tears stream down his face.

"Why won't you stay in court?" Christopher panted, "I could make you my right hand, isn't that enough?"

"It's not that I'm not satisfied," Timothy lifted Christopher onto the desk, filled with memorials, looking down at him.

Christopher, eyes wet and brows furrowed, asked, "Then why?"

Timothy caressed the tear-stained beauty mark by Christopher's eye, whispering, "I was never meant for officialdom. There's only one thing I want to do."

Christopher's heart pounded, "What is that?"

Timothy smirked, leaning in to whisper, "To conquer the emperor."

With that, Timothy thrust deep, hitting Christopher's sweet spot, making him scream, his abdomen convulsing as he climaxed.

But Timothy, consumed by desire, couldn't stop. He continued thrusting into Christopher, driving him to tears, his vision darkening as he neared unconsciousness.

Nicholas had been right; Timothy was indeed a brazen man.

Caught in the storm of their passionate love, Christopher thought with a mix of satisfaction and helplessness.

—-

Christopher had summoned Kalle back to Poiema.

With Bowie's execution and Queen Owen's imprisonment, Kalle, as her lover, was supposed to share her fate. However, remembering Kalle's role in helping him escape the palace, Christopher spared his life.

Back in Poiema, Kalle resumed his role as Crown Prince Vera's attendant.

The day after Kalle's return, Timothy visited him.

After months apart, Kalle's eyes filled with tears upon seeing Timothy. He hugged him, both laughing and crying.

After expressing their longing, Kalle couldn't help but complain. Now that Queen Owen's faction was eradicated, he hoped to leave the palace and serve Timothy, even as a scribe or stable boy. But fate seemed to keep them apart.

Seeing Kalle's despondence, Timothy comforted him, "Kalle, you've protected the emperor and earned great merit. Serving the Crown Prince isn't good enough? Why do you want to leave the palace to serve me as a scribe or stable boy? Has the Crown Prince mistreated you?"

"No, no!" Kalle quickly denied, "The Crown Prince treats me well, I just..."

"Just what?" Timothy asked.

Kalle furrowed his brow, looking up at Timothy hesitantly, "I can't really explain it, but I just don't like staying in the palace."

Timothy remained silent for a while, about to speak when a clear voice interrupted.

"Timothy!"

Turning towards the voice, Timothy saw a figure rushing out from the hall—it was Crown Prince Vera.

"Wow, Crown Prince, you've grown quite a bit!"

Palace life seemed to suit Vera, who had shot up several inches, now only a head shorter than Kalle.

"Timothy, you haven't changed at all. No, I should call you Lord Timothy now!"

Mature beyond his years, Vera spoke with a surprising air of authority for a child.

"Kalle, I heard what you said. You don't like staying in the palace, do you?"

Kalle's face paled, quickly kneeling, "Forgive me, Your Highness, for my thoughtless words."

"That's not what I meant!" Vera lifted him up, tears welling in his eyes. "Blake and Arya are gone. You're the only one left by my side. If you leave too, I'll be all alone."

Blake and Arya had been promoted for their loyalty, now commanding the inner guard.

"Your Highness..." Kalle, softened by Vera's vulnerable expression, said, "Kalle would never leave you."

Vera's eyes brightened, "Really? You're really staying?"

Kalle, caught between laughter and tears, could only nod.

A clever play on emotions, Timothy thought as he watched from the side, amused.

Kalle, born into a humble background and once a favorite of Queen Owen, must have endured many contemptuous glances in the palace. Vera, as the Crown Prince, paid no heed to Kalle's past and treated him with genuine kindness. How could Kalle not be grateful?

Moreover, Vera was indeed quite lonely.

Vera had once been accompanied by Blake and Arya, who were more like family after years together. Now, both brothers had been assigned to the Imperial Guard. As the Crown Prince, Vera could not leave the palace easily, and their frequent meetings became a thing of the past.

Before they left, Vera had asked Timothy to visit Blake and Arya on his behalf.

The next day, Timothy, carrying Vera's message and a jug of wine, visited the Imperial Guard camp outside the city.

"Is that Timothy?" Blake called out, spreading his arms as he approached.

"Congratulations on your promotion, Blake!"

Despite the time apart, their bond remained strong, and they embraced warmly. Arya stood behind Blake, watching the reunion with a cold expression, then cleared his throat. Timothy quickly added, "Of course, congratulations to Arya as well!"

"Why do you always make me seem like an afterthought?" Arya grumbled, glaring at Timothy, his usually icy demeanor showing rare annoyance.

Timothy widened his eyes, staring at Arya's face without saying a word.

"What are you staring at? Do I have something on my face?" Arya frowned, looking sideways at Timothy.

"No, Arya, it's just that you've never spoken more than ten words to me before," Timothy counted on his fingers, then pinched Arya's cheek, "Have you changed? Or is someone impersonating you? Addicted to disguises, maybe?"

Arya, embarrassed and angry, slapped Timothy's hand away, "You're the one who's addicted to disguises!"

Blake laughed heartily, "Timothy, you don't know, Arya may not talk much usually, but when he's in a good mood, he talks a lot."

Arya's face turned red and white in quick succession, "Stop talking nonsense, brother."

"Really?" Timothy's eyes lit up, "So Arya is happy to see me?"

Arya, unable to argue, waved his hand in frustration, "Say whatever you like. I have things to do. Excuse me."

With that, he turned and quickly walked away, leaving Blake and Timothy laughing.

After Arya left, Blake and Timothy sat under a tree, drinking and talking. Timothy conveyed Vera's sentiments to Blake, who sighed heavily after listening, "The Crown Prince has been very kind to us. Arya and I were more than willing to remain his attendants for life. But some things are beyond our control."

"Serving in the Imperial Guard is also protecting the Crown Prince. I'm sure he understands that," Timothy patted his shoulder.

Blake frowned, "Yes, Arya and I feel the same. I'm just worried..."

"Worried about what?" Timothy asked.

Blake took a sip of his wine, silent for a moment, then shook his head, "Nothing. It's probably just my imagination."

Blake's uncharacteristic hesitation sparked a bit of suspicion in Timothy. Just as he was about to press further, the sound of hooves drew their attention. Timothy looked up to see a familiar figure, clad in a crimson cloak, riding a tall horse and surrounded by soldiers.

"Penelope!?" Seeing the familiar figure, Timothy's curiosity was replaced by surprise, "What's he doing here?"

Blake replied, "You didn't know? Mr. Morris is now a general, overseeing the thirty thousand Imperial Guards, including us."

"A general!?" Timothy was astonished.

Penelope had indeed played a crucial role in the recent coup, but Timothy hadn't expected Christopher to place such trust and favor on him.

"Who else would the emperor reward, with you and King of Nixie refusing titles?" Blake said, patting Timothy's shoulder, "King of Nixie returning to Sunder is one thing, as a vassal prince staying close to the emperor could stir suspicion. But you? Refusing any official position despite your great contributions? Naturally, the emperor would reward Penelope. Besides, Penelope is of the Cypress lineage."

"That's true. Cypress was once a great general, so I suppose this runs in their family."

"Times have changed. Cypress's tenure as a general was marked by great glory, but Penelope has taken up a challenging role amidst chaos."

Curious, Timothy asked why. Blake, drinking his wine, began to explain.

Queen Owen and Bowie had controlled the court for years, depleting the treasury. When Penelope took over as general, he found that military funds had been severely embezzled, barely enough to sustain the thirty thousand Imperial Guards.

"You know there have been calls for reform, but no consensus yet. Mr. Morris had to take drastic measures, starting by cutting a portion of the old and injured soldiers."

Blake pointed towards the camp, where Penelope stood, reviewing the soldiers and making notes. Nearby, several soldiers, carrying their belongings, were leaving the camp.

"These are the surplus troops? But they don't look old or injured," Timothy observed.

"Though the Imperial Guard is elite, even slightly less capable soldiers are being dismissed. Mr. Morris said we need to cut at least half of our force to survive this winter."

"And where will they go?"

"Nowhere. They'll become street beggars or vagrants."

"Won't that cause trouble for the citizens of Poiema?"

"There's no choice; the court can't afford them."

Timothy had no words. No wonder Nicholas was so eager for reform; it seemed the court was on the brink of collapse.

"Timothy!"

Penelope approached, examining Timothy curiously, "What brings you here?"

Timothy, still holding Blake's shoulder, lifted the wine jug, "Visiting friends, and congratulating you, General Morris!"

Penelope squinted at them suspiciously, "Congratulate? For what?"

"Being appointed as a general, isn't that a big deal?"

"The title sounds impressive, but the pay is less than half of what I earned as the governor of Sunder, with ten times the responsibilities. I was freer in Sunder. If not for the emperor's sake... Forget it, let's not talk about these annoying things. You're just in time, come with me."

"Sorry, I'm busy now, I can't accompany you, General Morris," Timothy lazily waved his hand, turning back to drink with Blake.

Penelope bit his lip, then stepped forward, snatching the wine from Timothy's hand.

"What are you doing..."

Before Timothy could protest, Penelope tilted his head back, downing the remaining wine in a few gulps.

Timothy stood up, eyes wide, "Hey! You drank it all!? That was the wine the Crown Prince sent for Blake!"

Penelope raised an eyebrow, "What? The Crown Prince's wine isn't good enough for the general?"

"You...!"

Timothy was about to retort but was stopped by Blake, who laughed, "Drink as much as you like, General, as much as you like!"

Penelope wiped his mouth, tossing the empty jug back to Timothy, "The wine is gone. Now, will you come with me?"

Reluctantly, Timothy was dragged out of the Imperial Guard camp by Penelope, and stuffed into a carriage. Penelope sat beside him and instructed the driver, "To the western market!"

In Poiema, most nobles lived near the eastern market, where luxury goods were sold. The western market, frequented by foreign merchants, sold more everyday items.

The sun was high, and the market was bustling. Penelope walked briskly, with Timothy struggling to keep up, asking, "Why did you bring me to the market?"

"Other than buying things, what else would you do here?" Penelope continued walking, eyes fixed ahead, an air of casual nonchalance about him.

Timothy's curiosity deepened, "Aren't you General Morris? Don't you have servants for this? Why drag me along as your lackey?"

Just as he finished speaking, Penelope abruptly stopped. Timothy, unable to halt in time, crashed nose-first into the back of Penelope's head, clutching his nose in pain.

"You...!"

Timothy was about to curse when Penelope spoke.

"We're here." Penelope glanced back at Timothy, signaling for him to follow.

Rubbing his aching nose, Timothy looked up to see a fan shop.

"You want to buy fans?" Timothy entered the shop, glancing around in confusion.

Penelope didn't respond, instead leisurely examining the variety of fans displayed. After several attempts to get a response, Timothy gave up and leaned against the wall, feeling bored.

He was nearly nodding off when he felt a nudge on his arm. Opening his eyes, he saw Penelope standing before him, holding three fans.

"Wake up and help me choose. Which of these three is the best?"

Frowning, Timothy looked from Penelope to the fans, "You dragged me here to help you pick fans?"

Penelope remained firm, "Just choose."

Grumbling, Timothy took the fans: a simple and elegant paper fan, a flamboyant feather fan, and an embroidered silk fan with gold and silver threads.

Not knowing much about fans, Timothy figured someone like Penelope, with his high standards, would prefer the understated elegance of the paper fan or the luxury of the silk fan. The feather fan seemed out of place.

However, Timothy decided to be contrary. He picked up the feather fan, "This one."

Penelope's eye twitched slightly, "Why?"

Timothy explained with feigned seriousness, "Isn't it obvious? This one is the most beautiful. The others are just plain black and white. Boring! This one, though, is vibrant and unique. Look at this color, even greener than our neighbor's hat. It's like they say, surpassing the master! I think this suits you best."

Penelope scoffed, "Tacky."

Timothy grinned, "You just noticed?"

Despite his disdain, Penelope turned to the shopkeeper, "I'll take all three."

Timothy was baffled, "All three? Then why did you make me choose? What a waste of breath."

Penelope glanced at him, "Stop talking and pay up."

Timothy froze, "Pay? Pay for what?"

"For these fans, of course." Penelope crossed his arms, smirking, "Did you really think I brought you here just to help me choose?"

"Wait, wait!" Timothy grabbed Penelope's arm, pulling him aside, "Why should I pay for your stuff? What am I to you?"

Penelope's eyes widened, "Didn't the emperor tell you anything?"

Thoroughly confused, Timothy demanded, "Tell me what? What's going on?"

"The treasury is depleted. From now until the end of the year, everyone's salary is cut by half, including mine. But there's one exception."

Swallowing hard, Timothy felt a sinking feeling.

"The exception... is me, right?"

Penelope smiled, tapping Timothy's chest with the feather fan, "Timothy, the emperor is really, really fond of you."

Timothy shot back, "So what? My salary is mine. What does it have to do with you?"

Penelope replied calmly, "In tough times, we help each other out. Besides, this isn't a personal matter. We need to increase troops on the frontier this winter. I'm using half of my salary to fund the military, buying horses and equipment. By helping me, you're helping the Great Alvah court. In the long run, you're saving the people on the frontier. Still think your salary has nothing to do with me?"

"Nice way to twist things!" Timothy pointed to the fans, "So you're using your precious remaining salary on these frivolous things?"

"I love these frivolous things. They're my solace. What do you know?" Penelope rolled his eyes, extending his hand, "If you're a man, pay up without whining."

Timothy, half exasperated, half amused, muttered, "Is this how General Morris borrows money?"

But he still pulled out his money pouch and paid for the fans.

"Just this once, don't expect it again." Timothy glared at Penelope and turned to leave, but was stopped by a call.

"Wait!" Penelope approached, handing him the feather fan, "A gift for you. I never take from others without giving back. This green fan suits you."

With a wink, Penelope exited the shop.

"Hey! Take this tacky thing back. I don't want it!" Timothy shouted, chasing after him, but Penelope had already jumped into his carriage.

Peeking out from the curtains, Penelope waved, "Thanks for the company, Timothy. I'll remember this favor forever."

With that, the carriage sped away, leaving Penelope's laughter echoing in the street.

Timothy stood there, holding the green fan, unable to decide whether to keep it or toss it. Finally, he shouted in frustration, "I don't need your gratitude! I want my money back, with interest!"

In the evening, as Timothy stepped through the door, a tantalizing aroma of chicken soup wafted through the air.

The fragrance emanated from the backyard that adjoined the kitchen. Timothy made his way to the backyard and from afar, he could hear the sound of laughter and joy. A slender figure was bustling about in the courtyard, and it was none other than Adam.

Dressed in coarse linen that was convenient for work, Adam was chopping wood and carrying water, a whirlwind of activity around Timothy's parents. The master chef at the stove was Timothy's father, Edward Shaw, a man of few words but many talents in the kitchen. Despite his age, he was still particular about his cooking and maintained his daily routine in the kitchen.

In contrast to Timothy's father, Timothy's mother, Holmes, was born into a wealthy family and had an approachable personality. However, she had a habit of being clumsy when doing chores. Yet, she was a person who could not stay idle. Seeing her husband busy in the kitchen, she would always hover around restlessly, trying to help, but often ending up causing more trouble with her good intentions.

For these trivial matters, the couple often bickered and argued, which was a common occurrence for Timothy.

But ever since Adam arrived, the Shaw family had become much more harmonious. Adam was quick and clever, always eager to take on tasks. Whenever the couple was on the verge of an argument, he would naturally step in and subtly divert the conversation.

Over time, Adam gradually became the family's lubricant and the source of joy. Especially for Holmes, seeing Adam made her smile so wide that it seemed as if she had become ten years younger.

"If only Adam were a girl," Holmes often said, a remark she had made to Timothy on multiple occasions, and today, in front of Adam, she repeated it.

Chopping wood, Adam chuckled and said, "Holmes, couldn't Adam be your adopted son just the same?"

Holmes, picking through the vegetables, shook her head and said, "That's not the same. If you were a girl, you would be a daughter-in-law of the Shaw family, the kind with a proper marriage proposal!"

Adam smiled shyly, lowered his head, and said nothing.

Timothy felt a stirring in his heart and did not step out, but stood to one side, eavesdropping on their conversation.

"Adam, you're not young anymore, why don't I arrange a match for you?" Holmes suggested.

Adam looked up abruptly, shaking his head vigorously, "No, no, no, Adam has just turned sixteen this year, it's not yet time to settle down and start a family..."

Holmes laughed, "Ah, your Uncle Edward married me when he was fifteen, and I was already pregnant with Alan when I was sixteen. Why can't you settle down and start a family? Look, the daughter of our neighbor next door is just about your age, I think it would be better if..."

Upon hearing this, Adam became so anxious that the woodcutter in his hand fell to the ground with a clang, and he stood up abruptly, his oval face flushed red, stammering, "No, no, no, it's not possible!"

Holmes was puzzled, "Why not? It's not a loss to just meet her."

Adam was so anxious that sweat began to form on his forehead, and after stammering for a while, he couldn't utter a single word.

Timothy couldn't bear to watch any longer and strode out.

"Adam! So you're here, I've been looking for you for a long time!"

"Alan!" Seeing Timothy, Adam seemed to have found a savior and quickly grabbed his sleeve, "You're finally back."

Timothy smiled, "I brought something good for you, come, let's go back to the room and have a look." Then he turned around and deliberately spoke loudly to the bewildered Holmes, "Mother, look at how you're peeling these vegetables, the leaves are all pulled bald!"

"Ha!? Oh no, oh no!" Holmes looked down and inwardly groaned.

"How many times have I told you!" came Edward's unceremonious roar from the kitchen, "Don't be distracted when you're working, can't you understand or are you deaf?"

"I was trying to help you!? Good intentions are treated like donkey livers and lungs!"

Taking advantage of the old couple's argument, which left them with no attention to spare for them, Timothy grabbed Adam's hand, winked at him, and Adam immediately smiled broadly and ran out of the backyard after Timothy.

Timothy pulled Adam all the way back to the house, closed the door, and turned around to embrace Adam around the waist.

"Come on, give me a kiss, my Shaw family's properly married daughter-in-law."

Adam let out a gasp, his feet off the ground, blushing and pounding his shoulder, "Holmes just said that casually, joking."

"But I'm serious." Timothy kissed Adam on the mouth, "In my heart, Adam has long been a member of my Shaw family."

Adam shyly turned his face away, and Timothy's kiss fell on his neck, tickling him into a giggle.

"You're just flattering me with nice words, you have so many sweethearts, what qualifications does Adam have to be on the list?"

Timothy kissed his collarbone, "Look at what you're saying, where can you find such a virtuous and filial daughter-in-law like you, you've been with me for so long, don't you have this self-awareness?"

Adam laughed and pushed his head away, "Flattery is useless on me, the more impatient you are, the sweeter your mouth gets."

But Timothy did not allow him to escape, grabbed his hand, and put it into his pants, "With such a beautiful and delicious daughter-in-law in front of me, can I not be impatient?"

"You...!" Adam was just about to turn around in embarrassment when he was caught by Timothy and pressed against the door. Adam's slender wrist was tightly held by Timothy, and he was obscenely rubbed back and forth on the hard thing.

Adam said helplessly and with a smile, "You can't wait for such a short time? Dinner will be ready soon."

Timothy impatiently took off his pants and said, "Just help me with your mouth, I promise it will be over soon."

Adam couldn't resist Timothy, so he knelt in front of him, holding the thick thing and said, "Alright, but don't ejaculate on my face, otherwise, if the smell is left and uncle and aunt find out, it will be troublesome."

Timothy pointed the stiff thing at Adam and laughed, "That's not easy? You can swallow it all."

With time pressing, the two no longer hesitated to talk nonsense, and Adam was not the first time to perform oral sex for Timothy, he was already familiar with it. He first extended his hot tongue and licked the evil thing to make it shiny and smooth, then took it in and slowly swallowed it.

Timothy closed his eyes, frowned, and panted excitedly in bursts. At first, he just stood still, enjoying Adam's lips and tongue service. Later, he was aroused and couldn't help but reach out and hold Adam's back of the head, thrusting his hips back and forth in Adam's mouth.

The two were busy making love when suddenly there was a knock on the door, and Holmes' voice came from outside: "It's time for dinner!"

Adam was startled and reflexively wanted to let go, but was held by Timothy's head and pressed tightly to his crotch. The thick and long meat sword was deeply thrust into Adam's deep throat. Adam's eyes widened sharply, and in the strong nausea, his throat suddenly convulsed and contracted fiercely.

"Coming!" As soon as Timothy's voice fell, he couldn't help but shake the meat sword, and the sticky white mucus was sprayed out, pouring into Adam's deep throat in bursts. Adam was held by the head, unable to move or retreat, and could only helplessly close his eyes and let Timothy vent at will. The Adam's apple slid up and down desperately, swallowing all the thick semen.

When Holmes walked away, Timothy finally let go. Adam, who was finally relieved, knelt on the ground and gasped for breath. Timothy looked down at him and saw a line of white mucus inadvertently slipped from the corner of Adam's mouth, obviously the residual essence that was too late to swallow.

Timothy took out a silk cloth from his arms and gently wiped the white mucus from the corner of his mouth.

"I'm sorry, I still dirtied you."

Adam was not angry, just glanced at him, and said with a bit of anger: "It's very fishy in my mouth, what if I can't eat later, it's all your fault."

"Then... I'll help you rinse your mouth?" Timothy's mouth slightly raised, and said he lowered his head to kiss Adam's lips.

"Stop it! It will catch fire again!"

Adam hurriedly pushed Timothy away, wiped the corner of his mouth, turned red and ran away.

After a full meal, it was already night. Timothy sat by the window to keep accounts. He held a pen in his hand, and in front of him was a thick account book. He quickly played the abacus while writing and drawing in the account book.

And behind him, Adam was slowly and orderly making Timothy's bed.

"Alan, there's something I want to tell you." Adam lowered his head and said while tidying up the clothes.

"What's up?" Timothy didn't even look back.

"I want to go back to Tim County."

Adam said this naturally, as if he were talking about something commonplace. Timothy didn't react at first. He was stunned for a while before suddenly realizing what Adam meant. He turned around abruptly.

"You're going back to your hometown?"

Adam corrected him seriously, "Not hometown, my old home."

"What's the difference?" Timothy quickly put down his pen and pushed the ledger aside, moving closer to Adam. "Adam, are you angry? I'm sorry. I shouldn't have been so impatient today, forcing you to do that for me..."

Adam's face turned red with embarrassment. He pinched Timothy's arm, "I'm being serious here, and you're just messing around."

Timothy sat cross-legged beside Adam. "Not angry? Then why? Are you uncomfortable living in Poiema? Or is it because my mother keeps pestering you to go on blind dates and it's bothering you?"

"Holmes is a great man! Edward treats me like his own. I will be grateful to them all my life." Adam lowered his head, his eyes glistening. After a moment of silence, he said, "That's why I have to go back. Because every time I see them, I can't help but think of my parents..."

At this point, Adam's voice choked up, and large teardrops rolled in his eyes.

Timothy suddenly understood. Adam was homesick and missing his family.

"I get it. You want to go see your parents." Timothy put his arm around Adam's shoulders. "What's the problem? Are you planning to go alone? Or... should I go with you?"

Adam quickly shook his head. "This is my private matter. You have so many things to do in Poiema, so many people to see. How can I let such trivial matters distract you? Besides, I don't even know if my parents are still alive. If I make you come along and it's a waste of time, I'd feel even worse..."

Timothy looked at Adam with a complex expression, unsure of what to say for a moment.

Adam's understanding and thoughtfulness were his virtues, but his humble and difficult background had planted deep seeds of inferiority in his bones, making him always belittle himself.

Seeing Adam like this made Timothy's heart ache.

After a long silence, Timothy held Adam's hand and said softly, "Adam, your business is my business. No matter how small your matter is, to me, it's a big deal. From now on, don't say you're insignificant."

Adam agreed quickly, "Okay, I know."

But he knew that he would still act the same way next time.

Foreseeing such a future, Timothy felt helpless and could only sigh silently in his heart.

About the Author

Shuang Chenyue, a renowned author of female-oriented romantic fiction in China, was born in Nanning, Guangxi. After graduating from Sichuan International Studies University, she pursued her graduate studies in Japan at Doshisha University's Sociology Department in Kyoto. Upon obtaining her master's degree, she returned to China and currently resides in Shanghai. She is a VIP author on the Haitang Culture online literature platform, specializing in writing romantic fiction with themes such as martial arts, political intrigue, and fantasy, often set in an imaginary ancient China. Her representative works include "Unrecognizable him" and "The Beauty with Poison."

Read more at https://www.missevan.com/sound/3625999.

www.ingramcontent.com/pod-product-compliance
Lightning Source LLC
Chambersburg PA
CBHW021435150726
47989CB00001B/265